THE FAKE DATING TROPE

JENNIFER ANN SHORE

Print ISBN: 979-8-9859928-1-6

For Christine,
who would love My Alien King
just as much as Lucas does

ONE

Fifty-four steps.

It's the first thing that flashes in my mind when the bell rings its one-note chime that is a little too loud and goes on for a little too long.

I jolt at the sound, but the number and action that forms in my head brings me immediate relief, signifying how many times I need to put one foot in front of the other until I reach the library.

It'll be a quick jaunt as I navigate through the science wing, turn past the language arts classrooms, and avoid all other students until I arrive at my destination.

I move quickly, visualizing the glass-paned doors before I've made any headway in the hallway. Now that I'm thinking about them—manifesting them, really—I'm not sure they're glass. They might be some material I don't know the name of or could be coated with some protectant to withstand the years of abuse from thousands of teenagers.

Whatever, though.

That's not the point of all this.

I don't care about the treatment of the entrance of the space as much as I do the contents contained on the shelves—and the table wedged all the way in the back, which I long ago claimed as my own.

It's been neglected for a while, which is no surprise given that it's hidden behind rows of outdated encyclopedias and is one of the few areas without a window, but it's the perfect spot for me.

And at this exact moment, I'm forty steps from the threshold.

I pick up my pace as the warm and fuzzy feeling of impending familiarity surfaces, along with the desperate need for quiet among all the happy chattering, lockers slamming, and squeaking shoes on the tile floor.

"Kate!"

I wince at the sound of my own name and come to a stop mid-step.

It takes a tremendous amount of effort to swallow my groan as I turn and take in the sight of Zoe bounding down the hallway.

Her hair, piled on top of her head in some sort of intricate knot, makes her seem even taller than usual, and her long legs move quickly as she catches up to me.

I don't miss the handful of appreciative glances the sway of her dress earns her as she moves—it's short, but if I wore it, it'd hit below my knees.

But that's not what immediately catches my attention.

It's rare to see her without a smile; although, sometimes it's more devilish than gleeful, but at the moment, it's wide with unabashed excitement.

And I know from years of experience being her best friend that it's probably a bad sign she's wielding it in my direction.

"What are you about to try and convince me to do?" I ask, cutting right to the point.

"Nothing!" Her response is too quick and too innocent to brush aside. "Nothing at all."

"Uh-huh," I breathe.

Zoe wraps both arms around me, attaching herself like some sort of sea creature. She's without a single fleeting care that we're interrupting the flow of traffic as we take up too much space moving through it.

I, however, am getting itchy taking in all the glares and pointed huffs we're earning.

"Just tell me what you're plotting so I can say no and we can move on," I say quickly.

She gives me an exaggerated pout, which is painted with bright purple lipstick.

"Zoe." I give her my best warning tone. "Out with it or I'll throw you off and make a run for it."

"You're absolutely no fun," she says with a sigh.

"And you're rude," Daphne scolds as she catches up to us.

I'm instantly relieved by the sight of her—not just because she's becoming more of a friend to me with each passing day, but she might be the only person other than me who could say something like that to Zoe and get away with it.

"I'm not rude," Zoe argues, finally releasing her hold on

me to slip her hand into Daphne's. "I'm honest. If not a little grating at times."

I let out a laugh at that truth. "Well, at least you're self-aware."

Zoe smirks at me. "Among many other wonderful traits."

"Anyway, I'm off to the library," I say, eyeing an escape route.

We're nearing the point where I'll have to backtrack if I don't break away, adding more steps while diminishing those precious minutes I have to myself.

"No," Zoe whines. "Not today."

I was hoping the presence of the girlfriend she's all googly-eyed over would distract her from whatever nonsense she's up to, but I'm not that lucky.

"What's your deal?" Daphne asks her.

"I was merely looking to persuade my best friend in the whole wide world to join us for lunch this afternoon," Zoe answers. "You know, share a meal together and talk and stuff."

That's Zoe code that she has gossip or needs my help with homework—or both.

"No, thank you." It's the response I always give when she tries to get me to join them. "I need to recharge for a bit."

"But I want to spend some time together," Zoe presses.

I give her a skeptical look, one eyebrow cocked as high as I can muster. "Why?"

"Because it's been days since we've—"

"You forgot to do the English assignment, didn't you?" Daphne cuts in. "I told you not to waste your night with that stupid reality show. Everyone's just in it for the money and social media followers. It's not even real."

"It's not stupid," Zoe fires back. "People have found true love on that show! And, most importantly, *I* happen to like it."

Lines of irritation form on Daphne's forehead. "And we both know that *Kate* likes her time alone at lunch. So, why don't you look up the answers on your phone like everyone else and let her be?"

I give Daphne a nod of appreciation as I try to distance myself from them.

"Fine," Zoe says on a breath. "But if everyone is copying stuff online, it's going to be pretty obvious."

"That show must have really melted your brain if you think it's going to be difficult to reword some answers," Daphne teases as she pulls her in closer.

Zoe lets out a noise of annoyance that ultimately turns into a laugh, which Daphne quickly joins in on.

I bite the edge of my bottom lip, trying to withhold a smile.

It's moments like this where I don't mind being the third wheel to their relationship, mostly because it means my escape is imminent.

"See you later," I say before I awkwardly step between a few people.

I round the corner, momentarily unbothered that I'm still going against the normal walking pattern, and I don't stop moving until I'm officially in the library.

The sounds of my classmates yelling, telling jokes, and causing chaos in the halls lessens with each step I take toward my spot in the back.

Sometimes I wish I could fast forward past certain situations and moments that drag, and this is one of them.

I don't know if it's my eagerness to retreat into the pages of the new vampire *Pride and Prejudice* retelling or to devour whatever treat Aunt Marie packed for me today, but I can't get settled fast enough.

I cut through the fiction section, keeping my eyes locked on the turn I have to make, and once I do, I brighten at the sight of the old wooden table and two matching chairs, practically skipping as I take the final steps.

Of course, in all my eagerness, I don't spot the impending obstruction until it's too late.

Actually, I don't *see* it at all, but I *feel* my face smack right into a broad chest.

The mixture of shock and pain causes my reflexes to overcompensate, and instead of merely righting myself, I fly backward, knocking my head against the shelf.

The heavy books aren't impacted by the force of it, but my body is.

If it wasn't so mortifying, I might find the flailing of my arms—like I'm some sort of cartoon character—before I hit the ground amusing.

But I'm too off-kilter to do anything other than try not to cry.

"Oh, damn."

Those two words are an apt response, but they don't come from my mouth.

I squeeze my eyes shut briefly to compose myself, and once I've taken stock of the ridiculousness that just transpired, I glance upward.

Lucas Hunt stares down at me, grimacing at my current state.

It's really a disservice to the world that his mouth is fixed into a frown.

Because while I don't know him well, I have seen him enough in passing to know when he smiles—a genuine one—there's a shallow dimple that forms on his left side.

"Are you okay?" Lucas asks.

He crouches down, forcing me to meet his gaze and assaulting my senses with spearmint.

At least it's not a woodsy smell or sandalwood or whatever cliché is used to describe the male specimen in the books I can't help but be obsessed with.

"Are you bleeding?"

I gingerly touch the back of my head, wincing at the tenderness, but thankfully I find no broken skin.

"No," I tell him. "I'm not bleeding."

Externally at least.

Inside I'm dying just a little bit.

Metaphorically speaking.

Frankly, I'm just grateful that someone had the forethought to ensure that the rows of books couldn't fall with one shove because I'd never live down the embarrassment if I brought the entire section to the floor with me.

Lucas, however, appears to be very concerned. "Do you want me to take you to the nurse? Get some ice or something?"

"I'm fine," I manage.

I groan a little too loudly as I stand up, and he follows suit, reaching his full height and peering down at me with those still-concerned eyes.

My mind is already moving away from this ordeal and fixating on the details of him and how he's pretty much the opposite of me.

I'm on the shorter and, er, normal-looking side, and he's the pinnacle of an athlete with his tall stature and lean muscle composition.

Actually, I don't know if those are all requirements of someone who plays baseball, but it's who he is, and I hear he's good at the sport, so I'm going to roll with it.

We've been at the same school forever, but other than Zoe, Daphne, and the occasional in-class partner, my social circle is pretty small—unlike Lucas who usually has Sydney Smith hanging off his arm like an accessory when he's not accompanied by one of his many teammates.

This collision might be the first direct contact I've had with him.

And I'm not sure what precedent that sets.

I pick up my bag, which got dropped in the scuffle, and try to right myself back to normalcy by tugging down the hem of my shirt.

It's one of my many plain articles of clothing, which make up nearly the entirety of my wardrobe. I also have a few hand-me-down pieces Zoe gave me when she miraculously shot up four inches two summers ago, but my ensemble today is all my own from the Target discount rack.

I brush past Lucas to shuffle the short distance to my table, relieved to finally arrive.

The smell of slightly musty books that greets me with every inhale is the equivalent of white noise for my senses, and I look forward to reveling in solitude for just a little while.

Lucas, apparently, has other ideas.

His palms hit the back of the spare seat across from me, and my inner panic takes hold at the idea of him *joining* me here.

To my relief, he remains standing, but his hands flex in a way that makes the veins on his hands and forearms stand out.

And I immediately understand why that detail is one that authors specifically point out—along with a perfect cupid's bow, the hard line of a jaw, and a pair of gorgeous blue eyes, which, of course, Lucas also has.

It's a shame that this is reality and not a story contained in pages.

Life would be so much easier if I were some sort of mythical creature drawn to her mate, erasing all self-doubt and succumbing to the whims of lust.

"You sure you're okay?" Lucas asks, tilting his head in assessment.

I doubt his thoughts are in line with mine, and, to be honest, I'm surprised I'm considering him like this at all.

I must have *really* hit my head.

"Yeah," I exhale. "I'm okay."

"It's just…if I've learned anything, it's to not mess around with head injuries," Lucas hedges. "Serious stuff."

"I'm not 'injured,'" I retort. "I just had a little clash with a bookshelf, and it's not the first time."

I don't know why I tell him that.

But he takes it as an *in*.

"Yeah?" He manages to make his amusement clear with that one word. "You spend a lot of time here?"

"Yes," I murmur.

He crosses his arms over his chest, which does all *sorts* of things to his arm muscles.

I immediately avert my eyes.

In the spirit of giving myself something else to focus on, I pull out my slightly smashed brown paper bag and my book, hoping my uninvited guest will get the hint.

But as I arrange everything on the table, I realize the cover of the Austen retelling is more salacious than the books I usually bring to school.

Lucas doesn't comment on it, but I think I catch a flash of a smile on his lips.

"Well, uh, thanks," I say as I reach for my headphones.

I feel weird showing gratitude, given that he's done nothing to earn it, but I don't know how else to get rid of him.

"You're welcome."

Those two words are said quickly in response, but there's something *lingering* that I can't figure out.

It's like the air between us feels heavier or more expectant or just noticeable in a way that I normally wouldn't pay any attention to.

"Are you not going to lunch today?"

I shake my head. "I'm busy with other things."

"Busy?"

Lucas hovers, eyes dropping to my book once again as he waits for me to respond.

I don't, though, because I'm pretending to be fascinated by the worn squishy ear pads I hold in my hands.

"Well, I'll let you get to it, then," he adds after a beat.

I nod in dismissal, but I don't dare look directly at him until he finally retreats, watching him drag one of his long fingers along the spines—a gesture I force myself not to have an opinion on.

Instead, I pull my hair in a low ponytail at the nape of my neck, mindful of the spot on my skull that's definitely going to bruise, then I pull on my over-the-ear headphones.

They may not be sleek or fashionable, but they have well-worn padding that sits comfortably and muffles surrounding sounds.

I don't plug them in because I don't have the right type of converter for my phone, so they don't actually work, but they serve well enough as earmuffs.

It's a comfort thing.

One of the few I have in my life.

After multiple social interactions and too many sounds, my brain feels like it's gotten sensory overload, and I need this time to recuperate before I face the rest of the day.

Thursdays are extra long because I have the closing shift at Books & Beans, the little coffee and bookshop my Aunt Marie owns.

I'm very, very grateful that she's in my life for many reasons, including her flexibility in working around my school schedule to make sure I'm bringing in some money to save for college.

I do wish I could be like most seniors who are permanently casual and giving into a case of senioritis while counting down the months until we graduate.

But I think I'm too anxious to be so frivolous.

I'm also applying for as much financial aid and as many

scholarships as I can, and neglecting classes now and letting my GPA drop below 4.0 would only jeopardize my plans.

That said, since my homework is done—as far into the future as my teachers will allow—and the latest batch of applications has been sent off, I'm giving myself a breather.

I'm taking what's left of this lunch period to enjoy a snack and a steamy love story between a vampire and her human.

A bubble of giddiness surfaces in my chest as I lean back in my chair, delving into exactly what I hoped for.

To my surprise and delight, the savory pastry my aunt sent along for my lunch today contains spinach, artichoke, and cheese, and although the crust is a day old, it retained most of its softness. The treat is the perfect mix of fat, carbohydrates, and deliciousness to sink my teeth into as I read.

I try to take my time with the story—and my lunch—but I devour both in perfect symphony, reaching the end of the book just as the bell rings, reluctantly emerging from my blissful state.

I won't get another moment of peace until late tonight when I'm restocking everything and doing my closing duties at Books & Beans, but I don't dawdle.

I pull off the proverbial Band-Aid, shove my book back into my bag, and toss my garbage in the trash—only to nearly bump into Lucas once again as I move to exit through the double doors.

We do the whole awkward shuffle where one person tries to step, but the other person does at the same time because they're both waving at the other to move.

"You go ahead," Lucas says after three instances of this.

"It's fine." I adjust the strap of my bag on my shoulder. "You were here first."

He runs a hand through his hair, increasing the charming mussed look. "I'm being polite."

"Go, Lucas," I encourage, taking a step back.

"Well, if you insist..." Lucas presses on the door so it opens a few inches, then peeks out.

I balk at this gesture because from my vantage point, it seems like he's avoiding someone, but before I can come to terms with that observation, he slips out.

From the scant details I know about him, his behavior is out of character.

Though, I suppose if I'd spent the last half hour fixated on him, I would have realized he was voluntarily spending his lunchtime wandering the library instead of amid a crowd of people in the cafeteria, just like Zoe tried to coax me to do.

I like to think I'm somewhat observant and a decent judge of character, and, most of all, I know when to stay out of things.

But I can't help my own inner curiosity.

Why is Lucas Hunt, of all people, hiding out here?

And more importantly, why am I so interested in the answer to that question?

TWO

If I could write myself as a character, I'd start the chapter with waking up in the morning.

It'd be a slow awakening process, coming to consciousness with the gentle sound of birds chirping out the window, and I'd stretch, letting the sleeves of my silk pajamas caress my skin as I reluctantly rise from my pillow top mattress and pristine white bedding.

It'd be the perfect way to come back into myself and set the tone for the day ahead.

But in my current reality, I'm jarred awake by a loud banging on the front door.

I groan as I sit up because my back is pinched tight from the position I took on the couch last night—half on my side with one leg thrown over the back of it—and I'm still wearing yesterday's clothes.

I was so tired after the shift last night that I didn't even manage to trudge over to my bedroom, but I suppose my proximity to the front door is a good thing because I'm being summoned to open it.

If it was some sort of mass murderer trying to barge in, I'd be totally screwed, but I can only hope that given this is happening at six in the morning and they have the audacity to knock, I'm good.

I yawn as I move toward the door, and there's another round of what I think is the heel of a palm hitting the old wood.

If this continues for much longer, the person is probably going to pound a hole straight through the—

"Katherine! Wake up and let me in! I have to pee."

I cringe at my mother's slurred words as I unlock the dead bolt and unlatch the chain as quickly as I can.

"Sorry," I say as she brushes past me.

Her movement is more of a stumble, but she makes it to the bathroom just fine. She doesn't bother to close the door as she tugs down her skirt, and she lets out an elongated noise of relief as she settles on the toilet.

I'm so disgusted by the sight and sound that I run toward my bedroom and slam the door behind me.

I take a breath as I adjust to my own private space. It's small and sparsely decorated, but every inch is clean and organized exactly how I like it.

I've got a bookshelf for the few books I've taken home with me from work, a dresser that doubles as my night-stand, and a twin bed that's pushed as far away from the window as it can go.

When I was little and my dad was still alive, I had toys and treasures and actual decor that I'm pretty sure he picked out from some sort of mail-order magazine.

But he's been gone a long time, and when we ran out of the money from his life insurance policy, we had to start selling off everything that wasn't a necessity.

That kept us afloat for a little while as my mom flitted between jobs and disappeared for weeks at a time, but now, the late bill pay notices and dwindling belongings are a sign of the current state of affairs.

My mother once even tried to hawk my car, but Aunt Marie stepped in when I told her the keys were missing. She threatened my mother with a combination of taking legal action and calling the cops if she tried it again—since it's now registered in my name—and it's remained untouched ever since.

I'm just counting down the days until I can get out of here and go off to college.

I rub my eyes, trying to signal to my brain to move on from these thoughts, but they stick around until I hear the sounds of my mother stumbling to the living room.

With the assurance she's out of the way for my getting ready process, I head toward the bathroom, hop in the shower, and stand in the lukewarm water longer than I should.

I go through the motions of getting ready for school and take extra time to wash my hair, frowning at the fact that no matter how much generic vanilla shampoo I use, the lingering smell of coffee will never go away.

The truth is that I romanticize the idea of going away to college and being on my own next year, but I think I'm going to struggle even more than I do now.

I mean, with the stress of overdue bills and all my mother's issues, I doubt this house will ever be a place I can come home to, but there is something daunting about being out on my own.

As long as I ignore the terrifying amount of student debt I'm up against—not to mention the thousands of dollars in scholarship money I need to earn to help cover everything—it's exhilarating.

Going to Columbia, living in New York, and experiencing a life on my own terms are things I dream of at night.

The only control I have at this moment is over myself, and even then, I'm too often at the whims of other people —waiting on customers at work, navigating my friendships, completing school projects.

I long for independence.

That thought echoes in my mind as I finish getting ready and make my way to the kitchen, stomach finally awake and rumbling.

Unfortunately, there weren't any leftover pastries from last night's shift, so I settle for peanut butter toast for breakfast and…a peanut butter sandwich for lunch.

My direct deposit should hit at midnight tonight, allowing me to go to the grocery store tomorrow with what little I can spare from my account, and I'm making a mental list of what to buy.

I do all the shopping for my mom and me because if it were her responsibility, she'd come home with nothing more than bottom-shelf liquor and cigarettes. Those items are definitely not worth blowing her meager paycheck on, but it's her choice.

After the screaming fit I endured when I tried to point

that out last summer, I don't dare bring up the idea of making different choices again.

Generally, I do my best to avoid her, but it's hard sometimes—like at this moment when I need to adjust her position on the couch so she's no longer using my bag as a pillow.

And, even better, she's passed out with her skirt still around her ankles.

I shake my head as I shoulder my bag, then cover her with an old knit blanket that contains more holes than actual fabric.

It's better than nothing.

And with that reassuring thought, I head out for another *riveting* day.

It's a little chilly this morning, but I still drive with the windows cracked, appreciating the spring air and the sound of it whipping in my ears.

I coast down the windy, tree-lined roads with ease, long acquainted with every twist and turn and pothole to avoid.

In my eagerness to get away from my mother, I left a bit too early, so I decide to take the long way to school—only to immediately wince at the wasting of precious gas and regret the decision.

My car whines as I make a U-turn, pressing the accelerator to get me back up a hill. I hit the pedal harder, trying to counteract gravity—but it's having none of it.

Worse, the check engine light comes on, and just as my eyes flick to it, a burning smell reaches my nose.

I don't truly start to freak out, though, until I catch the sight of smoke in my rearview mirror, and I let out a string of curse words as I pull off.

If there's any blessing in this situation, it's that I've miraculously made it to a long and straight part of the road where I'm not in danger of someone flying around a corner and crashing into me.

My car is so old and janky that I have to open the glove compartment to pop the engine hood, which is situated in the back of my car between the back seat and the trunk. I've heard this is a common thing for fancy electric cars now, but my vehicle is a rust bucket from the 1990s that is barely holding on.

I don't even know what I'm looking for when I stare down at the engine, but it gives my inner panic time to blossom.

Because it's not like this is a simple scratch or a flat tire. It's something beyond my comprehension, and it's likely going to be expensive.

And I can absolutely not handle expensive—or even cheap—repairs at the moment.

I take a few calming breaths and call Aunt Marie, who is in the middle of the busy morning rush.

She still spends a few minutes talking me down and promises to call her friend who drives a tow truck when things settle down for her as long as I send her the location I'm waiting at.

I grab my bag from the passenger side and drop my keys in the cupholder, as Aunt Marie suggested, and I debate waiting for the tow truck to show or calling Zoe or Daphne to come get me.

I'm currently very much out of the way for both of them, and if they have to drive here to pick me up, they're going to be late.

Daphne wouldn't care about missing her first class, but her parents would be furious when they received the tardy notification, and Zoe loves the art class she has and would hate to miss it.

I rub my temples as I repeat those options over and over again until a loud, mechanical purr sounds from behind me, and I turn to take in the matte black paint job of a sleek sports car.

Like my vehicle, it's a two-door, but this one looks modern and kind of sexy—if it's possible to even say that about an inanimate object.

I expect the person driving to blow past me, but with impressive handling, the car veers and comes to a stop right in front of mine.

I hold my breath as the door opens—like it will lessen the shock of the appearance of the person I now recognize stepping out.

Out of all the people in the world, it's Lucas Hunt who has valiantly come to my rescue.

Because *of course* it is.

"Are you okay?" Lucas asks, giving me a once-over.

I lean back against the side, trying to come across as the textbook definition of nonchalant.

Internally, though, I'm furious—not only with my helplessness at this moment but at the fact that it's been less than twenty-four hours since he last asked me that question.

I very much do not enjoy how it makes me feel.

"I'm fine."

His nostrils flare as he approaches, and I can only

assume he's breathing in the lingering scent of *something* burning.

I don't know the cause, but I'm glad I pulled over before my car blew up.

"Transmission troubles?" Lucas wagers, quirking a brow.

I shrug because his guess is as good as mine.

"Want me to take a look?"

"A tow's coming soon," I tell him.

He nods, then tilts his head as he takes in exactly what he's looking at. "Is this an MR2?"

I follow the lines of his eyes, even though I've looked at this car hundreds, if not thousands, of times in my life. "Yes."

The corners of his mouth tick up slightly. "A '93?"

"Nope, 1995," I correct.

It's not shiny and new like what my friends and class-mates drive, but I'm grateful my dad bought such a reliable car all those years ago. It has an engine and four wheels, and it's served me nicely.

Well, until now.

"Any accidents?" Lucas presses.

"No, thankfully. Although there was a close call right after I got my—" I stop, remembering who I'm talking to, and purse my lips. "Why do you ask?"

"Twin exhaust," he continues, ignoring my question. "Guessing a V6 engine?"

"Uh, yeah? I think?"

"How does she run?"

"Until this morning, pretty good," I admit. "I mean, a

little loud when the engine is cold, but then the sound kind of peters out."

"That's a trait of these for sure."

"Oh?"

Lucas removes his baseball hat to muss his hair, then puts it on backward, and for some reason, that move makes my stomach do backflips.

"You, Kate, have got a baby Ferrari on your hands," he says reverently.

I narrow my eyes in disbelief at my slightly rusted ride. "Excuse me?"

"Cute nickname, huh?" Lucas knocks the toes of his Nikes against a tire that is probably flatter than it should be.

I always planned on selling my car before moving to New York, but I figured it wasn't good for anything more than parts—now, though, with Lucas's words, I'm wondering if I'm being shortsighted.

Or, rather, unaware of the value of what I have.

"It's not, like, a collector's item or anything, but for a person like me, it's cool to see," he says.

"A person like you," I repeat incredulously.

Of course, someone like Lucas and his own flawless ride finds mine to be *charming*, but I find his interest mildly insulting.

"Yeah. But if it's the transmission going, like I think it is, it's going to cost you."

I groan, pressing my palms to my eyes.

This is absolutely not the news I wanted or needed, even though he's telling me what I already know. I'm desperately pinching pennies to be able to afford my future, not putting it toward something I won't even need in the fall.

"You need a ride to school?"

I drop my hands and glance up at him. "What?"

"School," Lucas says, amused. "That place we go five times a week?"

I roll my eyes. "I know."

"So, are you coming?"

Irritation bubbles up in my chest at his question.

No—at his *intrusion* of my very vulnerable and weak moment.

Again.

"Why are you asking?" I retort. "Why are you even here?"

He balks at my attitude. "I just want to make sure you're all right."

My quippy reply dies on my tongue at how genuine he seems.

It's not exactly his fault that he's caught me off guard, and I guess I shouldn't deflect my helplessness at him.

"I'm fine," I assure him.

He doesn't buy it. "Do you really have someone coming to pick you up?"

"Yep, I'm good."

"Suit yourself." Lucas shrugs and fiddles with his keys. "See you around."

As soon as his hand hits the handle of the door, my phone vibrates, and I'm just about to give myself permission to feel relief—until I read the contents of Aunt Marie's message.

Tow truck's going to be about two hours, and we're still slammed right now.

I sigh, but I understand. *I'll get to school. Thanks for the tow. I love you.*

Love you, too. Sorry, kiddo!

I open my contact list again, trying to figure out who I'm going to bother with my predicament.

After running through the same very short mental list I did a few minutes ago, I know that, truly, catching a ride with Lucas is the path of least resistance.

But it doesn't make it easier to give in.

"Wait," I call to him.

He's already closed himself in and is likely seconds away from turning the key and drowning me out, so I somewhat impulsively dash over to the passenger side and wrench open the door.

"Tow not coming, then?" Lucas asks, lowering the volume of his music as I stick my head in.

"Not fast enough," I answer. "Do you mind?"

"No. I mean, we're both headed to the same place."

Physically, yes.

But mentally, emotionally, and everything else, I highly doubt it.

THREE

I twitch every single time my phone vibrates on the table, distracting me from my Chemistry homework and forcing my gaze back to my screen.

And, unfortunately, it's not Aunt Marie with news from the repair place—it's my gossip-hungry best friend who uses more emojis than letters in her text messages.

Why am I just now hearing that you got a ride from LUCAS HUNT this morning!!!???

Kaaaaate!!!

LUCAS FREAKING HUNT!!!

ANSWERMENOW

KATHERINEEEEEEEEEE!!!

LUCAS !!! HUNT !!!

I tap back over to Aunt Marie's message thread where my last text to her sits unread, likely lost to the lunch rush.

I'm so grateful to have her help, but it doesn't come without guilt—she does so much for me, and it seems like, outside of helping her out by being her employee, all I do is drag her down.

We've always been close, but after my dad died, things became strained between her and my mother. It's only gotten worse as the latter continues to spiral and come home drunk in the early hours of the morning.

I think the last time they talked, it was a screaming match in the kitchen that ended with me hiding in my room with pillows pressed against my ears.

That was before I found the headphones.

My phone buzzes again, and I sigh before I flip over to Zoe's latest message.

L U C A S!!! H U N T!!! T E L L!!! M E!!!!

I shake my head and am about to put her thread on mute as yet another message comes through.

Respond to me NOW or I'm coming to the freaking library. YOU CANNOT IGNORE ME FOREVER, KATHERINE CRAWFORD!!!!!

The use of my full name paired with her threat makes me wince.

The only thing that would be more annoying than her repeatedly interrupting me via text would be for her to show up here to quiz me in person.

Because, to be honest, Lucas Hunt is not on my mind at the moment.

Instead, it's the staggering transmission repair bills—not to mention the other issues that came up in my overdue inspection—that have been weighing me down ever since Aunt Marie relayed the early diagnosis from the mechanic.

I decide, for the moment, it's best to try and placate Zoe

with the simplest and most straightforward information possible.

My car broke down.

Her reply is instant. *OMG!!!! NO!!!!*

Lucas happened to be driving by, and he offered me a ride to school. I frown at my message, then follow it up once more to drive the point. *That's it.*

!!!!!!! Nothing else happened?

No. Nothing.

And that's the truth.

There was nothing remarkable about the ride to school other than the car itself, which was immaculately clean like it had been recently detailed. There was no visible trash or crumbs of any kind in the cupholder, and there was a very faint lemon scent that didn't overwhelm me too much.

And I guess I also did appreciate the volume of the music, which was up too high for us to have to make any small talk but not loud enough that the bass would cause pounding in my head.

I was also consumed with texting Aunt Marie and rapidly searching for any guidance on how much the repairs could cost.

But are you okay??? Zoe asks.

Yes. I'm okay.

But my bank account definitely isn't going to be.

I can only hope that the shop has some sort of payment plan or a miracle happens and the car starts running again on its own.

But, like, why wasn't I your first call??? For the accident and for the LUCAS?

I didn't want you to miss art. And it's not a big deal. It wasn't an accident. Just transmission troubles.

That Lucas expertly diagnosed in all of two seconds.

You're more important than any class, Katey baby!!!

Thank you. But please do not call me that ever again.

In response, she sends a winky face.

I shake my head as I drop my phone back in my bag, figuring I've earned a moment of reprieve from dealing with other humans.

I power through the rest of my Chemistry assignment, then dive right into my latest escapist read.

As an employee of a bookstore, I should probably have a preference for physical books I can curl up with and hold in my hands after lighting a candle to read by.

But I go through them too fast to make purchasing them an option.

I've been very pragmatic about what I use my Books & Beans employee discount on, so all the books on my shelf at home are either absolute favorites or copies that were damaged in shipping and couldn't be sold.

The libraries, both this one and the county one about ten minutes away, along with its app on my old tablet, have saved me. And with the discretion of a digital copy, it's nice to be able to read in public without anyone seeing the big sexy alien on the cover.

I'm not one to yuck anyone's yums, but I have to admit it did take me a little time to warm up to such steamy romances. I went from reading sweet teen fiction to progressively darker new adult and adult romances, and now that I've stumbled upon titles like *My Alien King*, I'm hooked.

It is a very unrealistic and sexy story—like pure sugary deliciousness for my brain and attention span.

The writing is simple, in present tense, and straightforward, so I barely even notice the passing of time, which means the author is doing their job very well, in my opinion.

I wolf down my peanut butter sandwich as I read about the clan of hunters from planet Eckdor. Their massive spacecraft is discovered late one night by a woman leaving the front office of a hydroponic farm. She's, of course, stunned by the eight-foot-tall aliens and tries to run to her truck to escape them, but they are too curious to let her get away.

It has the makings to be a horror story at first, but it's pretty lighthearted.

There are a few funny moments as the aliens all pile into the bed of the woman's truck, then she takes them to her house and eventually calls her friends for help—and, of course, the humans and aliens all quickly pair off.

There's a language barrier between the two groups until the initial woman falls for and sleeps with the biggest of the invaders, and when it becomes apparent that their connection is deeper than physical, they become mentally paired and can read each other's thoughts.

Despite the wildly unrealistic plot, I'm captivated.

I'm halfway through the book, blushing endlessly at the *hot* scenes of them in the bedroom...in the bathroom...and, at this particular moment, on the kitchen counter.

"Hey."

I startle at the interruption, abruptly jarred out of the

couple's passionate lovemaking up against a toaster oven, then clutch my tablet to my chest as Lucas approaches.

As my eyes track his movements, I have a terrifying flash of reader-insert where I imagine my legs wrapped around his waist as he caresses my chest and licks a line down my neck.

I take a series of quick breaths and remind myself that Lucas is a normal human in jeans, a clingy black t-shirt, and a backward hat—not a bright green alien with a tail at his back and a crown on his head.

Without my permission, Lucas moves my bag off the spare chair and sets it on the table before he takes the seat for himself, then smiles at me, flashing his white teeth in a way that could disarm me completely if I let it.

I, instead, choose to hold rigid as my heart comes back to a normal rhythm, and I make no sound, movement, or gesture in the meantime.

He clears his throat and leans back, getting comfortable. "So, you're probably wondering what I'm doing here."

He's right about that.

But I'm definitely not going to cop to thinking about him at all in fear that something else is going to spill out.

"In the years we've been in school together, I don't think we've interacted once," he continues. "But in the past day, we've bumped into each other a few times, and I'm starting—"

"No," I blurt.

"No?"

My interruption surprises even me, but I don't falter as I clarify myself. "We haven't 'bumped into' each other. You just keep showing up wherever I am."

Lucas bites the corner of his mouth, failing to suppress his smile. "Semantics."

I let out a huff of annoyance, then put my tablet to sleep before I turn toward him, hoping the sooner I give him my full attention, the faster we can get this over with.

"What do you want?" I ask plainly.

He gives me a look of complete seriousness—eyes squinting, jaw tight, and brow hard. "To date you."

I jerk so hard that my shoulder blades smack the back of my chair. I let out a small yelp, and the pain reverberates so deeply I wouldn't be surprised if I find bruises there later.

Lucas frowns. "Are you—"

"Don't ask me if I'm okay," I snap, then take a breath before I speak again. "What are you talking about? Dating me?"

"I'm interested in a relationship of convenience," Lucas explains.

His words are even, without a hint of teasing or sarcasm, and I have nothing to offer back to him.

I'm literally stunned into silence.

It doesn't help that he picks this moment to push his sleeves up on his forearms, which—as any good romance reader knows—is like kryptonite for some reason.

"You heard how much your repairs are going to be?" Lucas asks, resting his elbows on his knees.

I close my eyes briefly, grateful that he can't sense my line of thinking, and shake my head. "Probably a lot."

"I also noticed your state inspection sticker is from three years ago, so who knows what you're in for with that," he continues. "But my best rough guess is you're looking at over five grand for parts and expenses and labor."

I haven't gotten the final quote yet, but hearing him say that number out loud is physically painful.

"Really?" My voice has definitely lost some of its punch. "You think so?"

"I know so," Lucas says confidently. "My dad owns H&H Repairs, and I called and spoke to Don, the manager, who told me that—"

"You did *what*?"

He waves me off, like there are more important concerns for me to focus on. "So, as I was saying…dating."

"What about it?" I grit out.

"You need a car, and I need a girlfriend."

"You *need* a girlfriend?" I echo in disbelief.

He tugs at the neck of his shirt. "Yep."

"This doesn't make sense."

"It's a mutually beneficial arrangement," Lucas insists.

"What about Sydney Smith?"

His lips tighten briefly before he answers. "We broke up months ago."

I blink. "Really? I didn't know that. I mean, I feel like I *just* saw her hanging on your arm the other—"

Lucas cuts me off with a wave of his hand. "This is why I need a girlfriend."

My mind races as I process his line of thinking, and I just want to make sure I have complete clarity at this moment.

I press my palms flat on the table. "Let me get this straight. You want me to date you, and if I do, your dad's just going to waive the fee for my repairs?"

"No." For the first time, a flash of something other than lightness appears in Lucas's eyes. "Screw that guy. I'm going to fix it myself. For free. Well, free to you."

"All for me to…date you?" I say slowly.

"To *pretend* to date me," Lucas amends. "I mean, no one would know it's not real except you and me."

I drop his gaze, slightly stunned by this information.

My eyes fall to my tablet, which is innocuously sitting there, waiting for me to pick it back up and dive right into delicious storylines like—

"Oh, no," I groan as I renew our eye contact. "You didn't just do that."

"Do what?"

"You did *not* just propose the fake dating trope to me."

Lucas's brows pinch together. "The what?"

"The fake dating trope," I huff, holding up my tablet. "Two people start fake dating, then find out they're actually perfect for each other, but they're too stubborn to see it until it blows up in their faces."

Lucas has the audacity to laugh. "Let's hope our situation is far less angsty and dramatic than that."

I press my thumbs to my temples, rubbing them in circles as I process his offer. "This is…a lot."

"It's really not," he scoffs, scooting forward in his chair. "It'll take me a few weeks, two months tops, to get your car fixed, and in that time, we can…date. For show. An even trade."

"Two months?" I repeat in exasperation. "Why so long?"

Lucas rubs the back of his neck. "I have some tools in the garage at home, but I'll need to take a look at the extent of the issue to know what parts to order, then we have to wait for them to come in. And I'll do the actual work."

I suppose that timeline works out where we'll be together long enough to make it believable but not trapped to each other for prom and graduation and all those moments that people want to have last a lifetime.

Really, it's the perfect window of opportunity—we could time a breakup to happen over spring break, and then I'll be back in the Toyota right before I turn eighteen.

The cost savings and ability to cruise right into adulthood would be the best gift I've ever gotten.

Which all sounds too good to be true.

I swallow, then let out a breath. "And you'll just…fix it? But you're not even a professional. I mean, what if you make it worse or something?"

"Oh, come on," he says jovially. "Your car will practically be brand new by the time I'm done with it, and all you have to do is be seen with me in public. You're getting the better end of the deal."

"If that's true, then why are you pushing this?" I ask curiously.

Lucas bites the edge of his mouth. "I just—"

"Hey, Kate, are you back here?"

Before I can even respond, Daphne turns the corner and comes to a stop at the sight of Lucas and me at the table.

His posture of ease coupled with the way I'm leaning toward him gives the illusion that something more intimate is happening than our back and forth.

"Hey," I say as casually as I can.

I try to adjust my body into a normal position, but now

that I'm conscious of it, I'm overthinking it, sitting up unnaturally tall and holding my arms stiffly.

"Hi," Daphne returns in a slightly suspicious tone.

I force a smile at her. "What's up?"

"I'll get out of here," Lucas says as he stands. "I've got to talk to Coach before the bell anyway."

Daphne and I both watch his retreat—although I'm sure we're thinking vastly different things.

"But just think about it, Kate," he adds, turning back briefly. "Okay?"

"Okay," I promise.

Because there's no chance in hell that I'm going to be able to get lost in my steamy alien romance now that I have a real-life book trope to consider.

"I didn't believe it when Zoe told me," Daphne says, taking the chair that Lucas vacated. "What are you doing talking to Lucas Hunt?"

"We're not *talking*," I protest.

Daphne quirks a brow. "Just getting rides to school and having secret meetups in the library?"

"There are too many plurals in that sentence," I deflect.

She taps her fingers on the table in irritation. "You're being excessively coy."

I sigh and tuck my hair behind my ears. "Well, you're being…you."

That makes us both laugh.

As our chuckles peter off, Daphne gives me a look that I really don't want to decipher.

"I don't know what you're up to, but if you need me for anything at all, I'm here for you," she says gently. "If you don't want to tell Zoe, I'm a good second choice."

I smile, and it's genuine and gracious. "I appreciate that."

"And as a person who is very invested in your well-being, I should warn you that not only is Zoe not going to let you off as easily as I did, but if Sydney Smith gets wind that you're hanging out with Lucas, she's probably going to threaten your life."

I let out an exaggerated groan, but I keep the handful of curse words that come to mind inside.

"Do you know how long it has been since they broke up?" I ask her. "Or any of the details?"

"That's a question for Zoe, and you know it," Daphne teases as the bell rings. "But if you want details from her, you're going to have to offer up some of your own."

"I know," I admit sourly.

"Life's just a series of trade-offs, Kate."

"You have no idea how true that statement is," I grumble, gathering up my stuff to follow her out.

FOUR

I don't think I'm a judgmental person.

Not in the traditional sense, anyway, where I'm overly critical—it's more like I just want to understand things and the motivation behind an action.

For example, I don't particularly enjoy eating spicy food, finding the act of getting sweaty over a meal or reaching for a water glass after every bite taxing. But I've tried enough hot sauces to understand the depth of the flavors and what they can contribute.

It's not for me, but I get it.

Right now, though, I'm desperately trying to understand the appeal of baseball.

Not only that, but I'm curious as to why anyone would show up to watch a *practice* of the sport as opposed to an actual game where there's food and some sort of action.

There are quite a few people in the stands around me, content to watch the team run drills around what looks like a ladder made of rope, and I can't figure out the draw.

I guess it is a little comforting to not be completely alone here or drawing attention to myself, but the occasional whooping and clapping is loud and sporadic enough that it becomes an annoyance.

There's one guy in particular who keeps *whistling*, and the sound makes my entire body itch—not just when he actually does it but in the quiet beats when I'm anticipating him making the sound again.

As much as I would love to escape into my book, I'm too fidgety, so I lean into one of the techniques Ms. Molinaro, the school counselor, suggested the other day —meditation.

At first, I scoffed at the idea because I'm not the type of person who finds activities such as yoga to be anything other than a test of my patience, but she got me to try it.

And I found it actually a little bit helpful.

I try to replicate what she guided me through, focusing on my breathing and silently naming every single muscle and bone in my body I recognize, taking time to reassure myself that everything is okay.

I don't know how long I do this, but eventually I come out of the *zone*, feeling lighter and able to focus on how the sunshine feels on my hands with ease.

When I finally open my eyes again, ready to process my reality, I see that the players have split into small groups around the field.

To my untrained mind, it seems a bit disorganized how everyone's paired up—some with bats, others with gloves —but they're all laughing and seem to be enjoying themselves, even as the coaches yell for them to refocus.

Naturally, I'm drawn to Lucas's movements.

It's definitely only because I'm waiting for him to notice me so we can talk after he's done and *not* because I find that the oddly cut baseball pants look flattering on him.

Lucas stands in the large, grassy area, that I overhear other people referring to as the "outfield," about twenty feet away from his teammates.

He twirls a baseball bat in one hand like he's some sort of magician before suddenly tossing a ball in the air. As soon as it's right where he wants it—though how he might determine that I have no idea—he swings, sending it flying over to his teammates.

This process repeats exactly twelve times before a coach jogs over, and they spend the rest of practice adjusting his stance and hitting more blurs of white into the air.

Overall, it seems like a lot of standing around and very slight milling about, and I think if they cut out all the excess, practice would be condensed into fifteen minutes instead of two hours.

Eventually, the players and coaches high five, signaling the end of the session, and my original question surfaces: What about this is appealing?

I don't get it.

Some of the people around me must be parents or relatives of the players, heavily invested in their futures, but I also recognize a few of my classmates—including Sydney Smith, who is flanked by a group of her friends.

I wonder if they're all dating someone on the team and she's tagging along or if she's here just to watch Lucas.

More importantly, if Lucas and I go through with this whole fake dating thing, am *I* going to be expected to show up?

I'm late for work, which Aunt Marie is cool with for now, considering my circumstances of the day and lack of transportation, but I have better things to do in the afternoons than be stuck here for hours.

"Good practice, Lucas!" Sydney calls as the players make their way back to this end of the field.

His expression is pinched as his eyes dart in her direction.

And as a reflex, I give him an exaggerated wave, trying to catch his attention before he can run away.

He blinks in surprise at my presence and gesture, then gives me a small smile.

I lower my arm as he trades his cleats for a pair of slides, grabs his bag, and heads toward the locker room.

I take his hurried movements as a signal that he'll be right back, so I don't bother joining in the staggered departure of everyone else.

Instead, I settle in as best I can on the uncomfortable metal, hugging my bag to my chest and kicking my feet up on the row in front of me.

When Lucas emerges twenty minutes later, the field and most of the parking lot is empty, and I'm grateful for the privacy to continue our earlier conversation.

"Hey," he says, dropping down beside me.

I inhale the mild scent of his shampoo, appreciating the spearmint scent that doesn't seem overly manufactured. "Hey."

"I assume you're not just here because of your sudden love for America's favorite pastime?"

I snort. "Do people really say that about baseball?"

He smiles as his gaze wanders over the field. "I do."

"Oh." I wring my hands on my lap. "Well, uh, yeah, I wanted to talk about your proposal."

"You're accepting?" Lucas smirks as his eyes lock with mine.

I've gone through many potential scenarios and the potential fallout, but it's almost too easy to accept because I am absolutely *desperate* for the free car repairs.

I'm scraping by as it is. I can't afford to drain my account.

And, honestly, after reading about relationships for so long, part of me is curious about experiencing one.

Even if it's fake.

"I have questions, though."

"Understandable," Lucas says. "Ask away."

"And conditions," I add.

He props his feet up at the same time he leans back on his elbows, taking up three rows of bleachers with his long limbs. "Hit me."

"Why are you doing this?" I ask plainly. "Really. Not just a surface-level answer."

"I want to send a clear message to Sydney that we are no longer together."

"That's kind of ridiculous, isn't it? You can't just, I don't know, *talk* to her?"

Lucas gives me a look of irritation. "I have. Talked and talked and talked. For months. Avoided her. Blocked her on social media, but she keeps making burner accounts or having her friends look up what I'm doing. She comes to most of my practices, and she's come by my house a few times. It's just…I don't know what else to do."

I don't have any experience with romantic relationships,

but this—her level of attachment *and* the length he's willing to go to send a message—does sound like kind of a lot.

"And what do you expect me to do? Be a human shield?" I frown at the idea of that and what follows. "I mean, has it occurred to you that instead of obsessing over you, she may channel that energy into making my life hell?"

The way he runs his hand over his face makes me believe he hasn't thought of that.

"I'd really love to not contribute to some narrative of women hating other women," I tell him. "The world has enough of that."

"Is your life just one big book?" Lucas asks playfully. "Are you writing scenes and romanticizing every little detail?"

"No," I answer. "I'm just saying that if she sets my hair on fire in AP Chem, you're going to have to do a lot more than fix up my old Toyota."

He lets out a genuine chuckle. "Fine. What else do you want to know?"

I sigh as I relent. "How does this whole thing actually work? We just one day tell the world we're dating? Get someone to read it on the morning announcements?"

"You know, if your tone wasn't so condescending, I'd think you were actually pretty funny," Lucas says. "In a very sarcastic kind of way."

"You're not ensnared by my charms, then?" I say as evenly and dryly as I can.

Lucas shakes his head. "Nope."

"Well," I breathe, straightening my posture. "That can be one of the things that contributes to our breakup."

He rolls his eyes, but I can see he's fighting a smile.

If I'm being honest, I am, too.

"I think we should go for subtlety," he muses. "Be seen together and let people speculate."

"That seems like a pretty loose plan."

"You have a better idea?"

"No." I laugh a little. "Not in the slightest."

"Well, for starters, I think you should come to my games."

I groan at that. "I can be present, but do I have to pay attention? I mean, I'm not trying to insult you, but I just find this stuff to be so..."

"Long?" Lucas suggests.

"Boring," I declare.

"Wow," he breathes. "My own girlfriend doesn't support me."

I should fall into his teasing tone, but I'm caught up by that word and hearing it come out of his mouth in relation to me.

Girlfriend.

I'm somebody's girlfriend.

Then I rub the bridge of my nose with my forefinger and thumb, sending a signal to my brain that this is exactly what I need to remember—and avoid.

I am his *pretend* girlfriend.

None of this is real.

I'm just trying to get my car fixed, and he's trying to move on with his life.

"What else?" I ask, a little strained. "What else do I have to do?"

I'm trying to stick to the facts and form a checklist in my mind of exactly what this all entails, aiming to simplify this complicated situation.

"You should let me walk you to class," Lucas says matter-of-factly. "Especially Chemistry. We could even eat in the cafeteria on—"

"Nope," I cut in. "That's a hard no for me."

"Really?"

"I need my private library time."

"But it'd be perfect."

I shake my head. "Not negotiable. Can't do it."

"Fine." He sighs. "Where else might we be seen together? Where do you usually go?"

"Work," I supply. "And, uh, home."

"Great."

I tap my fingers on my bag. "I know I'm not the most exciting person, but it's the truth."

"Could you find something more public? See if any clubs can take late sign-ups. I know the French club did that last semester so people could pad their college applications."

"I don't speak French."

"Well, find something you *can* do. That way I can, like, support you."

"Lucky me," I say under my breath.

But he doesn't miss it.

"It'll be great," he insists.

Lucas is making a valiant attempt at trying to earn some shred of enthusiasm, but I'm not buying it.

"I don't think anyone's going to believe this, Lucas. I mean, we just suddenly start dating out of nowhere? Come on."

"That's why I suggested *subtlety*," he reminds me.

"You keep using that word without giving me a solid idea of what you actually mean."

He snorts. "Let's start by exchanging phone numbers."

It seems like a fair suggestion, so I rattle mine off for him to put in his phone, then he does the same for me.

"That's what you're going to save me in your phone as?" Lucas asks, clearly put off as he reads over my shoulder. "'Lucas Hunt.'"

"Is that not your name?" I deadpan.

He holds up his phone and shows me where he's typed *Kate* followed by a kissy face emoji. "See?"

"If I ever send that emoji to you, assume it's a sign to call an ambulance."

"It's *my* choice, not yours," he counters. "You've got to get a little more personal."

Just to be petulant, I add the standard smiley face—the most generic of all the options—after his name.

"Nice. Actually, here..." He scoots closer and slips his arm around my shoulders, then holds up his phone.

"What are you doing?" I demand, pushing away from the selfie in progress.

"We should post a picture together," he says, pressing the button just as I give him a look of irritation.

"I thought you wanted to be subtle."

"Obviously," Lucas bites out. "Which is why a casual photo will do the trick."

"I agree with you on principle but not execution," I tell him.

His expression blanks. "Huh?"

"That photo is not going to have the effect that you hope."

"Why not?" Lucas holds it up like he's trying to get me to see something I'm missing. "It's cute! You're looking at me with adoration."

"That is *not* my adoration face."

He purses his lips as he glances at it again. "I guess you don't exactly *have* an adoration face."

"How would you know?" I retort, raising an eyebrow.

"Fair point."

"Look, I may not know much about how all this fake dating and social politics stuff works, but I can tell you, as soon as you post that photo, Sydney is going to send it over to her friends in a group text and tear me apart." I pause, ensuring he's taking my words seriously. "That's the type of photo a scorned person mocks. Not one they silently seethe over."

Lucas sinks his teeth into his bottom lip as he considers this, then after a minute of silence, he perks up. "Okay."

"Okay?" I repeat slowly.

"So, you tell me, then. What should we do? What kind of photo sends a clear message? And induces enough jealousy from the greater population that it's clear we're together?"

It's my turn to contemplate his words, and I think about what exactly makes me swoon so hard in some of the books I read.

The forearms, obviously.

Slight grazes.

Thighs touching.

And, damn, he's right—it's subtlety.

"Push up your sleeve," I order.

"Like this?" Lucas asks, tugging the material halfway up.

I let out a huff of irritation as I shake my head. "Just let me do it."

He mumbles something about impatience, but I brush it off, focused on setting the perfect scene.

I take care to reveal that objectively sexy forearm and rough hand of his, pleased to find that the tightness of the jersey he's wearing makes his veins pop even more.

I move closer to him, then prop my leg up on the bleacher in front of me. I flip the camera around, ensuring that my lap is in focus with the field in the background, and put his hand on my thigh.

I stare at it for a beat, then slide his palm more, and a little closer to my hips, going from friendly—if thigh-touching could ever be considered that—to intimate.

I pull his thumb away from the rest of his fingers, posing it like he's on the brink of a caress, then angle the phone so the photo is captured just as I envision in my mind.

"There," I declare, incredibly proud of myself.

He looks at the screen, then back at me.

And I force myself not to appreciate the amusement in his eyes or the way his mouth ticks up at the corner, revealing his very slight dimple.

Alarm bells go off in my head, and I shift away from him, letting his grasp fall.

I clear my throat. "So, there you have it."

He stares at the picture for a little too long. "I get it."

"Pure sexual tension meets breathtaking anguish," I say longingly. "Forever simping a modern Mr. Darcy."

"A what?"

"Never you mind." I shake off my own romantic notions as I glance down once more, then gasp at the time. "I'm *so* late for work."

Lucas stands and slings his bag over his shoulder. "I'm guessing you need a ride?"

"Oh, uh, yeah," I say. "I do. If you don't mind."

"Come on," Lucas says, leading me toward the parking lot. "You need a lift home later, too?"

"I should be good. I think I can get rides to and from work, but getting to school will be more tricky. I'll have to figure out the closest bus stop and the schedule."

He chuckles and shakes his head. "I'll pick you up."

"You'd do that?" I ask as I open the passenger door. "Play chauffeur?"

"I think it's perfectly reasonable for me to want to spend as much time as I can with my new girlfriend," Lucas says, sliding into the driver's seat. "Not to mention I'd get to show her off first thing Monday morning after people have been speculating all weekend about whose leg was in that photo."

"Brilliant," I admit. "And I'm sure the repair place is closed now, but I'll call tomorrow and see about getting my car over to your house."

"Already taken care of," Lucas dismisses, turning the key in the ignition.

I balk at his words. "Really?"

"Yeah."

He does that totally unnecessary thing where he puts his arm on the back of my seat as he glances behind us to back up.

I close my eyes for a beat, hating that everything he does is pretty much storybook-level attractive.

"I just figured you wouldn't be able to resist your own personal 'fake dating trope,'" Lucas says.

I glare at him.

Even though he's right.

FIVE

For the first time in my life, I understand the addiction and appeal of social media.

It's not that I'm a digital recluse—I just spend most of my time on book-related apps and posting photos when Zoe bullies me into doing it, which is why the ones I have are mostly of her.

But now I have a *reason* to be on there, and as a result, I'm looking at the picture Lucas posted for what is probably the millionth time.

I definitely have better things to do—working at Books & Beans means there's always some sort of chore, cleaning, or prep work to be done—but it's one of our slow hours.

And I can't help myself.

In the past two days, it's racked up nearly five hundred likes and a bunch of comments, ranging from heart emojis to people being snarky.

Judging by the screenshots Lucas has been sending me from conversations with his friends, it's a success.

"Whatcha looking at?" June, a very nosy and sweet ten-year-old, asks as she skips across the checkered tile floor.

Jessica, her mother and the bookkeeper and assistant manager, doesn't normally work on the weekends, but she and Aunt Marie are busy preparing for the tax deadline, so it's all hands on deck until they push it through.

And June, apparently, wanted to tag along.

She's spent most of the morning picking all the M&Ms out of a cookie while lost in some middle grade fantasy book.

Now, though, right in the dead zone of the day, while the adults are locked away in the back office, she's decided to strike up a conversation.

I'm more than happy to play along.

"This is what I'm looking at," I say, turning the phone to show her.

She scrunches up her nose as she stares at the image. "Why?"

I laugh at her skepticism. "Because it's of me and my…boyfriend."

It's my first time testing the word out loud, and my delivery is painfully awkward.

I guess it's a good thing I'm practicing on someone who doesn't understand the weight of what I'm saying or romanticize little gestures—because tomorrow, I'm sure I'm going to have to face all that head-on at school.

"You have a boyfriend?"

"Uh-huh."

"Oh." June grips the edge of the counter so she can leverage her body weight to hang and kick her feet.

Jessica has told her one thousand times not to do that,

but I'm not going to scold her. I'm not June's mother—and it's something I definitely would have done at her age.

"What color is his hair?" June asks suddenly.

Given that hers is bright purple, I suppose it's a natural question.

"Brown," I answer.

"Boring." June sighs. "Does he play hockey?"

I shake my head. "Nope. Baseball."

She stops her fidgeting and smiles wide. "Like, for the Pirates?"

"Not yet," I say with a laugh.

I actually have no idea if he wants to continue playing after high school or if he even watches the professionals. I mean, I would assume so, but I should probably learn that —along with a bunch of other information about him—in case people ask.

Then again, I'm not sure who's going to confront me about such details.

My social circle is pretty small, and I doubt hordes of our classmates are suddenly going to rally around me just because Lucas and I have started holding hands in the halls.

I wipe my palms on my apron at the thought.

"My sister is dating a hockey player," June offers. "He's really good."

I know this already because June talks Violet up every chance she gets, as does Jessica. I get a little pang of jealousy over their very sweet family dynamic every time.

"Yeah?"

"And my sister's best friend plays women's hockey," June adds before pausing. "Don't you think it's stupid that women's sports have to say *women* in front of it, but men's sports are just what it is?"

"I've never considered it before," I admit. "But, yeah. You're right. It's a stupid qualifier."

"Yes! So, your boyfriend..." She gives me a pointed and questioning look.

"Lucas," I supply.

"Your boyfriend Lucas plays *men*'s baseball," she says with a flourish.

I laugh at her seriousness. "I'll be sure to use that from now on."

"Good." June seems very proud of herself as she looks at the display case. "Can I have another cookie?"

"Sure. Same kind?"

She shakes her head and points. "I think I want to try that one."

I use the tongs to arrange the peanut butter cookie with the little crisscross pattern on top of a plate for her, then she skips off, back to her table and her book.

If I had a sister, or any siblings, I think it'd be nice to have someone like June—funny, kind, independent, and bookish —but it's just me at home with my absent single mother.

She's got her own stuff she's working through, I understand that, but as grateful as I am for Aunt Marie, sometimes I long for more of a familial unit.

I can't help but be curious about what that's like, and it's a strange connection, but maybe that's why I love reading romance books so much—there's a guaranteed happy ending with a front-row seat to two people falling in love and weaving their lives together.

I hope someday in the future I can find a *real* relationship like that, not a fake boyfriend who is using me as a shield in exchange for car repairs.

As a distraction, I pick up a rag from the disinfectant bucket and wipe down the already spotless counters, then I organize the little stands of stickers and bookmarks.

Aunt Marie calls this the "last-ditch effort" area because after most patrons have grabbed a book from the shelves that line the space, they eye the odds and ends we have on display as they wait for their coffee and usually end up buying something.

I seem to be immune to their charms because my bookmark of choice is usually a receipt or a piece of scrap paper, not a cute little decorated rectangle with a tassel on the end.

I run my fingers over them all, tracing the little floral patterns and characters depicted as I rearrange them to my liking. Just as I finish fixing the selection, the bell chimes above the front door, and I glance up to greet the incoming customer.

It only takes me a half-second to realize how wrong I was earlier—I don't have until tomorrow before everything comes to a head.

It's happening right now.

The hard line of determination on Zoe's features is as intimidating as it is foreboding.

"Katherine," she says evenly.

Daphne trails in behind her, wide-eyed and shaking her head in silent warning that I'm in for it.

I immediately decide to play dumb.

"Hey," I say brightly. "I didn't expect to see you two today. Want a chai latte or a peanut butter—"

"No," Zoe cuts in.

I press my lips together and wait for the impending verbal beatdown.

"You know why I'm here," she charges on. "Don't try to distract me with caffeine and baked goods."

"I'll take one of those, though," Daphne says, eyeing the chocolate scones.

Zoe glares at her before turning her attention back to me. "What I *really* want is for my best friend to tell me why I just received this picture from Amanda Gorski along with a message asking if those were *my* jeans!"

I busy myself with warming up Daphne's treat, using the movement to hide my wince.

Because I am, in fact, wearing a pair of Zoe's old jeans in the photo Lucas posted.

I was so focused on the mission that I forgot about the distinctive hole on the side of the knee—a result of her once tripping in the school parking lot.

"You think I wouldn't recognize that uniquely placed rip and the knobby-ass knee sticking out from it?" Zoe accuses.

"I don't think my knees are *knobby*," I say defensively, glancing down at my legs, even though they're contained in a pair of faded black pants.

"Not the point," Zoe fires back.

"I know," I groan, offering the plate to Daphne.

"Thanks," she says, testing the temperature of the scone with her finger before picking it up. "Zoe, just say what you need to say, and let's get on with it."

Zoe purses her lips as she watches Daphne sink her teeth into the pastry. "You think you'd be more understanding, given that I just found out through *someone else* that my best friend is getting *felt up* at the baseball field!"

I roll my eyes. "Felt up? Really?"

"Are you talking about that photo?" June asks from her table, not bothering to look up from her book.

Zoe's glare softens as her attention shifts to the little girl. "You've seen it?"

June shrugs as she turns the page. "I don't see what all the fuss is about."

"You will when you're older," Zoe insists.

"Are you jealous that Kate's boyfriend plays men's baseball?" June asks.

Zoe grinds her teeth as she turns back to me. "Boyfriend?"

"Thanks, June," I mumble.

"Explain yourself," Zoe demands, pointing a manicured finger directly in my face.

I let out a strangled exhale. "Lucas and I are kind of... dating now."

Zoe, for lack of a better word, shrieks.

And in a swift motion, she grabs me by the wrist, leads me around the counter, then practically throws me down into the seat across from her.

"I'm working," I say with a scowl. "I can't just sit around and chat."

Daphne snorts and gestures to the empty shop. "I'm sure all the customers waiting in line will be fine."

I turn my gaze on her. "Snarky patrons don't get the employee discount."

"I'm just as interested as Zoe is in how you're going to explain this," Daphne admits, brushing the crumbs off her fingers. "I'm simply more tactful about it."

"Enough stalling," Zoe says, drumming her palms on the tabletop. "Tell. Me. *Everything*."

I tug my fingers through my hair, squeezing the ends at the back of my neck as I try to decide where to even begin. "Uh..."

"Did something happen when he drove you to school?" Daphne prompts.

"Kind of," I admit.

"A real damsel-in-distress moment," Zoe swoons, abandoning her anger in favor of adoration.

"Well, the day before that, we bumped into each other in the library. I mean, he was in my way, and I didn't see him, and then he, like, lingered—"

"Ooh," Zoe breathes. "A romantic, longing type of vibe."

"I guess," I say. "Then he showed up again and, uh, asked me out."

Oddly enough, I don't feel bad about the mistruths I'm telling.

I doubt this situation between Lucas and me is going to have any sort of lasting consequence, so I roll with it.

"Then I went to his practice," I say, gaining momentum. "And then we talked and snapped the picture, and that's about it so far."

"Already social media official," Zoe says with a happy sigh, leaning against Daphne. "Our little lady is in love."

I choke at those words. "We barely know each other."

"Who cares?" Zoe says flippantly. "I mean, I'm not even

allowed to *visit* you during your sacred library time, but you're okay with him being there? That's a pretty big sign of early success."

"I don't think I'm exactly on board with it," I say. "It's more like I've endured it, and now this is where things stand."

"That's the point of dating." Daphne's tone is infuriatingly gentle. "To get to know each other."

At the very least, I'm grateful for the plausible explanation of why I barely know anything about the guy who is supposed to be my boyfriend.

"What do *you* know about Lucas?" I ask Zoe.

She practically bounces in her chair, eager to share the gossip she's collected. "He's *so* dreamy."

"Really?" Daphne says in amusement.

"What?" Zoe returns innocently. "It's true. And aside from Sydney Smith, I think the only other person he dated was that girl Kim who moved away sophomore year. I haven't heard why or when he and Sydney broke up, but now that I think about it, she's been giving him these longing looks in the cafeteria ever since we came back from Christmas break."

"He said they've been broken up for a few months," I supply.

"Already opening up to you?" Zoe waggles her eyebrows.

She's a little too smug for me at this moment, and I let out a sigh.

"I also heard that his parents are in the middle of a divorce," she continues with a grimace. "As far as I know, it's *messy*. Apparently, Amanda Gorski's mom was getting her oil changed at Lucas's dad's shop, and he and Lucas's mom were yelling at each other in the back."

I frown at her words.

What Lucas and I have at the moment is surface-level, and this information seems pretty serious. I'm not sure I've earned the right to have it.

But it does now make sense that he'd want to fix my car himself instead of having anything to do with his dad.

"Did you know he's going to Rutgers next year?" Daphne asks, polishing off the remainder of her treat.

"An easy commute for you two if you stay together," Zoe inserts.

I blink. "What?"

"Aren't New Jersey and New York right next to each other?" Zoe pulls out her phone and opens Google Maps. "Yeah, it's right on a train line, too."

"Good to know," I say noncommittally.

"And *far* shorter than our commute," Daphne says.

Zoe pouts as she reaches over to squeeze her girlfriend's hand. "Absence makes the heart grow fonder. So, maybe distance does, too?"

Daphne chuckles as she shakes her head. "Whatever you say."

Zoe is off to California in the fall, using school as an excuse to be in close proximity to Los Angeles and hopefully get scouted by a modeling agency, and Daphne earned a full-ride to a school in Virginia.

They've had it all planned out for months—how many times a day they're going to video call, which weekends someone is flying out, and all sorts of other factors that will ensure the longevity of their relationship.

And it makes me very aware of how much catch-up work Lucas and I have to do in planning our own relationship, even though our situation is very temporary.

Daphne and Zoe were friends for years before they started dating, while Lucas and I have had exactly three conversations.

Tomorrow in the car on the way to school, I'll drill him, and then I'll show up to his games, like we agreed, and I'll have to find something—

An idea hits.

"Hey, can people still join the Rainbow Alliance this late in the school year?"

"Yes," Daphne drawls skeptically.

"Cool." I smile brightly as I stand. "I'd love to join."

"What?" Zoe breathes. "Really?"

"Uh-huh."

"But you've turned us down every time we've tried to get you to come to a meeting," Daphne reminds me. "You're *always* working on Wednesdays."

"I've been at every single event, though. Well, when I haven't had a shift."

"And we appreciate it," she says immediately.

"Maybe I can switch shifts with the new hire or work something out with Aunt Marie," I say, thinking out loud.

"Aren't you going to miss out on tips from the 'Millennial Moms' book club who comes in every week?" Daphne asks.

I frown at that thought. "I am."

Because every single damn penny counts at this stage.

I don't like it, but I know that, rationally, a few weeks of this isn't a drastic change—and I am saving a ton of money with this entire arrangement.

So, why not?

"I'll work something out," I say reassuringly. "So? Can I join?"

They exchange flabbergasted looks.

"Have you had a personality transplant?" Zoe wonders aloud. "First a boyfriend, now a change in that rigorous schedule of yours—"

"Of course you can join," Daphne cuts in. "We'd be lucky to have you."

"Great," I say, resuming my spot behind the counter.

"They say being in a relationship shouldn't change you as a person," Zoe teases. "But look at you, already wanting to *participate*."

"I guess things will be different moving forward," I say with a shrug.

I have no idea just how true that statement will prove to be.

SIX

"Good morning," Lucas calls, voice a little deeper than usual at this early time of day.

I'm not exactly a morning person, so his enthusiasm as he steps out to open my car door for me is pretty grating—or maybe it's the fact that he looks absolutely gorgeous in his perfectly fitted jeans and tight, long-sleeved shirt.

It's not exactly logical to compare our appearances, but I'm running on a few hours of very unsatisfying sleep, so I'm being extra critical of my faded gray t-shirt and yet another pair of Zoe's hand-me-down jeans.

They're more recent, too, which means I've had to roll them up at the ankles to accommodate for our height difference—and I have no idea if it's a good look.

It's even more grating that I suddenly *care* about stuff like that.

"Morning," I grumble, slumping into the seat.

Lucas chuckles as he shuts the door, then swings around to let himself in. "Not awake yet?"

I shake my head, watching him buckle in and shift into drive. "Not really."

My mom and some of her friends came home in the middle of the night, and they weren't quiet about it.

She's not around much, and when she is, she's usually wreaking havoc on my life and the house. I never have any idea what state it will be in when I get home, but after coming back from work on Christmas Eve to find two of her friends passed out in my bed, I put a lock on my bedroom door.

So, that's one less thing to worry about, I suppose.

Frankly, I'm just glad everyone stayed asleep as I crept out of the house this morning—at least *someone*'s getting rest in that place—and, from the quick scan I did, they all appeared clothed.

My first ever glimpse at a naked man in person was when one of my mom's friends walked into the bathroom while I was brushing my teeth one day, but I've managed to mostly purge it from my mind.

I try to avoid all conflict—and my mother in general— and it's never been more true than now.

The last thing I need is for her to suddenly take interest in my life when Lucas and his very sleek sports car show up to cart me off to school each morning, so I let out a breath of relief when we turn off my street.

"Here." He pops the lid on his travel mug as he offers it to me. "Drink this."

I stare for a beat—at his fingers, their calluses, and his offering.

"You're giving me your coffee?" I ask.

"I'm *sharing* it with you," Lucas corrects. "I'm pretty amped up as it is, but my mom made it for me."

I can't recall anything my mother has done for me other than being a total pain in my ass and a source of worry.

"She doesn't really like that I'm drinking coffee," he continues. "But she says if I'm going to do it, it might as well be 'the good stuff.'"

"That's very sweet, actually." I accept it from his grasp and inhale the combination of coffee, vanilla, and hazelnut, then take a sip. "Oh wow."

It's legitimately delicious—rivaling the lattes and cappuccinos I make at Books & Beans—and I appreciate the jolt I get from the caffeine.

All it takes is one drink to send the message to my body to wake up.

"You approve, then?" Lucas asks in amusement.

"I do." I take another sip, then hand it over. "Thank you for sharing."

"Of course."

He tilts it back, taking a generous drink himself.

I'm frozen, watching his lips touch where mine just were—it's so casual yet so intimate that it makes me squirm internally.

"It's the least I can do for my girlfriend," he adds.

Just like the coffee I swallowed, his use of that word gives me a little zap.

And the sensation intensifies when he clears a drop of the milky coffee from his bottom lip with his tongue.

I wring my hands on my lap as I gaze out the window. "About that...I think we should, like, get to know each other a little better. I mean, we're social media official, but I don't know much about you aside from your knowledge of cars and the fact that you play the most boring sport in the world."

He presses a hand against his chest like I've wounded him. "Dating my biggest hater."

I roll my eyes. "Seriously, Lucas."

"Fine. Fine. What do you want to know?"

"When did you start playing? Are you going to keep it up in college? And you're going to Rutgers, right?"

"Woah," he says with a laugh. "Slow it down a bit. One question at a time."

I clear my throat. "When did you start playing?"

"It started with tee-ball," Lucas says. "Which I think was maybe kindergarten? Then rookie ball. Then fast-pitch. Then I started doing traveling teams before I made varsity my freshman year."

"Impressive."

"Not to you. But yeah, I guess, to some people."

"What position do you play?"

"Left field."

"That's a whole job?" I ask with a frown. "You just stand there and wait for someone to hit a ball your way?"

Lucas takes another sip before he hands the mug back to me. "It's a little more complicated than that."

I trace the rim with my thumb because now that I've mentally clocked the fact that we're practically kissing through coffee, I can't bring myself to keep doing it.

My first kiss—even if it's pseudo—will *not* be via a drink someone's mother made for them.

"And to answer your other questions, yes, I'm going to Rutgers," Lucas tells me. "Not to play. Well, not now. I was recruited, but I ended up liking the campus so much that I decided to go there even after I declined the scholarship."

"Someone was going to *pay you* to go to college, and you turned it down?" I say in disbelief.

"When you put it like that, I sound like an asshole."

I put the mug in the cupholder, then cross my arms over my chest. "I'm not saying that."

He sighs as he musses up his hair. "I hope not."

There's an awkward beat of silence when I don't contribute anything else to the conversation.

The coffee was good to shake off the remnants of sleep, but since I drank it on an empty stomach, it's making me jittery and a little irritated.

And deeply jealous.

Of his mom making him coffee. Of his ability to *turn down* a free ride. Of a car that works. Of his stupidly perfect exterior.

"It was just something that my dad always wanted for me, and it took me a long time to realize it wasn't something *I* wanted for me." He lets out a long exhale before he steers the conversation away from his future and over to mine. "What are your plans for after graduation?"

"Working until I leave for school," I answer, a little clipped.

"Where?"

I glance over at him. "Columbia."

"We'll be neighbors, then."

"That's what I hear," I mutter, tapping the toes of my sneakers together.

"And what do you want to study?"

"Something with books, I guess."

Lucas nods like my response comes as no surprise to him. "Like, writing?"

"I don't know."

I chew on the inside of my cheek, knowing that he doesn't deserve the brunt of my irritation, and I decide to open up and give him information to work with.

We are stuck together after all.

"Book-adjacent, maybe. I'm not the best writer, but I love to read. And edit. And I'm sure there are, like, a million jobs I don't even know about. My aunt has to coordinate with distributors and has even had a few publishing houses schedule readings and signings at Books & Beans."

"So, you hate baseball, and I hate to read," Lucas says, tapping the steering wheel as we idle at a red light. "Not great for our relationship."

"This was your idea," I return petulantly.

"I know."

I rub my upper arms. "But I don't think you don't like to read. It's more likely you just haven't found the right book yet."

"Oh yeah? What do you think would be the 'right' book?"

I think about it for a minute. "I mean, I personally love a good slow-burn romance—"

"What does that mean?"

"That the main character and her love interest spend a lot of the book tossing witty dialogue back and forth, getting to know each other, and have several *moments* before it all culminates."

"Kind of what we're doing right now, then?" Lucas bites the corner of his smile.

I reluctantly let out a chuckle, feeling the redness spread on my cheeks. "We're not bantering, we're...establishing. We need to learn these things so that you can get your ex off your back and I can get back to driving myself around."

"Right, right, of course," Lucas says.

"So, with that in mind, we should really work on our backstory," I press. "I already told Zoe and Daphne about the library situation and the car breaking down."

"But you didn't tell them the details?"

"I didn't think you'd want me to do that."

"Correct," he says. "Best to keep the whole truth between us."

"The whole truth and nothing but the truth," I recite immediately.

Lucas smiles at me genuinely with that dimple cutting in.

I clear my throat. "So, what had you so enthralled that you just *had* to ask me out and share a picture of us with the world?"

"You mean after you dove into me in the library and almost knocked yourself out?"

"Ugh. Stop."

Lucas laughs at his own joke as we pull into the parking lot. "We got to talking."

"About what?"

"I was looking for some book recommendations."

"In the encyclopedia section?"

"Stop poking holes in our own love story," he chides. "You're supposed to be helping. In fact, if you're going to be 'book-adjacent,' shouldn't you be the one making the decisions here?"

"Fine," I relent. "We *mutually* accidentally bumped into each other. You saw what I was reading, and you were so infatuated with my intellectual prowess that you couldn't help but ask me out right there on the spot."

Lucas nods as he puts the car in park. "Checks out."

"And after you picked me up on the side of the road, I couldn't resist your genuine offer to help or shake the idea that we could really be something."

"Then you came to my practice, and we made it all official?"

"Well, you could add some pizzazz to that, but yes."

"Cool." He checks himself out in the rearview mirror before he smiles at me. "You ready?"

I glance out the window, noting how some people wave at Lucas as they drive by, clearly recognizing his car.

Various groups and stragglers mill around the parking lot and along the benches that line the walkway to the entrance of the school—and I'm a little overwhelmed by the idea of purposely catching their attention.

"Come on," Lucas says as he opens my door.

I didn't even notice him get out of the car and circle around, but I accept his grasp as I stand.

He grabs my bag from the area by my feet and slings it over his shoulder along with his own.

"Should we hold hands?" I ask, taking a tentative step forward. "Is that something two people in a relationship would do on the walk into school?"

He tilts his head, mouth pulling to one side as he

assesses us together. "Actually, I think you're the perfect height."

"For what?"

He shifts our bags to his other side, then wraps his arm around my shoulder.

It's kind of a friendly gesture at first until he pulls me into him, and I have to keep my balance by pressing our hips together and sliding my hand around his waist.

It takes us a few steps to sync up, but we quickly go from awkwardly bumping into each other to falling into the same stride.

"Now you can hold my hand," he offers, wiggling his fingers in front of my face.

I shake my head and smile as I loop my fingers in his, holding them just in front of my chest.

His hands are rough, but I don't mind the warmth radiating from his skin to mine.

And then we have our *moment*.

It's the one I've read about and watched in movies so many times—when the couple walks hand in hand through a crowd and everyone separates to let them through as the camera pans.

At least, that's how it feels in my head.

In reality, we earn a few curious stares and whispers—no doubt fueling the fire of speculation on Lucas's posted photograph—before we make our way through the front doors.

I shrug him off just a bit to step through, but he presses his hand against my lower back, pinkie sliding against the centimeter of bare skin that's exposed.

"I'm just so infatuated with you that I can't keep my

hands off you," he murmurs low enough that only I can hear. "I can't help myself."

I could melt into a puddle of lovey-dovey goo if this were real.

And that's the kind of feeling and behavior I need to not fall into.

I can't be a victim to this situation—I need to take charge and control the only thing I can in this situation.

Myself.

And how I'm going to handle Lucas.

I don't know where I pull the boldness from, but I turn suddenly to press my hands against him, one on his chest and the other holding onto his belt loops, then glance up to meet his gaze.

"Likewise."

Something flashes in his eyes at my words.

But despite all my romance-reading, I can't associate the look he gives me with one emotion in particular.

Maybe a combination of surprise, impressed, and amused?

I try to catalog it, along with the way he's looking at me, but the moment between us is shattered as we get a reality check.

"Kate!" Zoe's tone is equal parts shocked and delighted as she and Daphne approach.

I drop my hands from Lucas as I turn, facing our first test.

"And Lucas," Zoe adds, smile wide as her gaze moves between him and me.

"Hey, Zoe," Lucas says. "And Daphne. How's it going?"

"Great," Zoe chimes in immediately. "So, so, so very great."

I press my lips together, unsure what to do next.

"We're getting numbers for this week's Rainbow Alliance meeting, Kate," Daphne inserts quickly. "And just wanted to confirm that you were really down?"

"Nice choice of club," Lucas says genuinely.

"Allies are welcome," I answer.

"I know. I've heard." He flicks his hair off his forehead. "I just thought you'd pick a boring book club or some Shakespeare fan group or something."

I balk at that. "Is that even a thing at this school?"

"I don't know. That's your area, not mine."

"Maybe we could add some required reading to RA," Zoe suggests, quirking a brow. "I mean, surely we can dip into your discount at Books & Beans, right, Kate?"

I shrug. "If you really want to, yes."

"Will you be joining us also, Lucas?" Daphne asks pleasantly.

He smiles at her. "When are meetings?"

"Every Wednesday after school."

"Ah, I have practice, unfortunately."

Zoe lets out a sigh and crosses her arms on her chest. "Lame."

"Is there another fundraiser coming up?" Sensing my look of confusion, Lucas adds, "Daniel said it was fun."

Daniel Fullerton is Lucas's best friend and teammate, and I'm dreading that official introduction, if I'm being honest, because he's pretty loud at all times.

"Unfortunately, that was the last one of the year,"

Daphne tells him. "But we did well. Casino night was a hit."

"Are there any other events this year?" Lucas asks.

Daphne shakes her head. "Just the prom stuff."

"Some kind of photo section, right?"

"Yeah. You heard about that?"

"I saw the posters," he answers.

"See?" Zoe says, elbowing Daphne. "I *told* you those would work. We should make more in our next meeting."

"My schedule is kind of grueling these days, but I'll try to make a guest appearance if I can," Lucas says. "Just can't stay away from this one."

He shifts to hug me from behind, and I jump in surprise, earning a laugh from the three of them.

"All right, all right," I say, slowly stepping out of his reach before glancing up at him. "Walk me to first period?"

"Happily," he says, winking at Zoe and Daphne before I tug him away.

I can *feel* their eyes on our backs as we walk.

"Well done," Lucas praises me. "Now that we've made our big entrance, it'll get easier from here on out."

I desperately want to believe him, but something tells me this is just the beginning of our complications.

SEVEN

"Hello, Kate," Ms. Molinaro says brightly.

"Hi," I return from my spot in the doorway.

I've been lingering for about ten seconds, trying to mentally prepare myself for whatever's about to happen.

Because it's a bit of a gamble when I step into this room.

I suppose I shouldn't feel any level of anxiety when stepping in the guidance counselor's office, but I've spent more time here over the past four years than most of my other classmates, so I'm relatively at ease.

It all started with a quick meeting to discuss my future and planning after those career aptitude exams freshman year, and it's since devolved into a bit of a planning and therapy session.

I'm taking free mental health care wherever I can get it.

"Come in, come in."

I step into her office, giving the familiar space a once-over.

It's a pretty small room, tucked away in the administrative department of our school, but she's taken care to make it homey—well, as much as one can make a windowless, white brick room feel that way.

The furniture is the same terrible brown color scheme that fills almost every room in this building, but instead of being accented with cheesy inspirational posters, she's plastered colorful artsy pictures of flowers all over most of the walls. Those, along with a purple rug, various trinkets on her desk, and a vase of fresh roses, complete the uniqueness of her office.

I'm usually very picky about my surroundings and how they affect my comfort level, but I actually don't mind the light floral scent or how cramped it is in here.

Ms. Molinaro maintains a bright smile as I take a seat in front of her desk. "How's it going, Kate?"

"Good."

It's generally the truth.

Because the past two days of pressure from dating Lucas hasn't been too much. Mostly I've just been getting whispered about when he and I walk through the halls holding hands and stared at by Sydney across the room in AP Chem.

And there's no news on the home front that's out of the norm.

Really, it feels like a regular old week with the exception of being called in here.

"You submitted the applications for those scholarships we reviewed last time we met?" Ms. Molinaro asks, gaze flipping between her computer screen and me.

"Yes."

"All...ten of them?"

Even with financial aid, I'm still about fifteen thousand dollars short of what I need to cover just one year of tuition at Columbia.

I've already been through the mental gymnastics of how reckless it was to fall in love with a very expensive private university in one of the world's most expensive cities, but I still have to dampen my own mental chiding at the thought of it.

After saving about half of that working minimum wage at Books & Beans, Ms. Molinaro has been throwing every single scholarship opportunity my way, even the ones that make up a measly few hundred dollars.

Every penny counts.

And she's been kind enough to help.

"I sent them in the week I got them," I tell her. "Now just waiting for someone to drop a pile of money at my feet."

"That's great." She beams as she toggles her mouse. "Because I have a new one for you for five grand."

I love when people casually address large sums of money flippantly. Like, *oh, just five grand...*

"I think you can tweak a previous essay you used about the vitality of creativity and nail it," she continues. "Maybe cater it to New York, though, because this is a state-specific one."

"Thank you," I say genuinely. "I'm really grateful for the help."

"It's my job," she reminds me.

My phone buzzes, and I check to confirm that I received what she sent. "Got it."

"Good." Ms. Molinaro pushes her keyboard aside so she can lean her elbows on the desk. "How's everything else?"

"Okay, I guess."

She tilts her head in assessment. "Did something happen?"

I press my palms against my thighs, and the warmth of my skin through my jeans is an instant reminder of Lucas's hand there when we sat on the bleachers.

I swallow.

My mind flashes with all things *him*—our fingers twined together or him slinging an arm around my shoulder, and he always makes a big show of holding my bag for me.

It's been...nice.

So much so that it's become a habit to reach for him, which I actually *do not* find that great.

I don't need an addiction. I need him to hold up his end of the bargain.

As promised, though, he has ordered the parts he needs to fix my car, and he's given me progress updates on their shipping times when he gets notifications on his phone— and despite his insistence at being *seen*, he's left me alone for lunch, which has been a nice reprieve.

"Kate," Ms. Molinaro says, voice tinged with concern. "Is everything okay at home?"

I blink at her pinched expression.

Right.

She's talking about my mother and her myriad of issues —actual things of consequence and not my pretend relationship—that I've written sparingly about in my essays.

"It's the same," I admit. "Counting down the days as I always do."

She lets out a sigh before offering me a tight smile. "You're a strong woman, Kate."

I know she's right.

I *am* strong and determined, and I am going places—with or without help—but it's kind of nice to hear someone else say it and know they truly believe it as much as I do.

Aunt Marie gives me plenty of love and affection, but it doesn't really count since we're related.

I'm sure there's something in her brain that signals to her that she's supposed to care for me given that I have roughly a quarter of her DNA.

A few years ago, she even made a play for custody, but my mother magically got her shit together, which lasted only as long as it took for her to keep me.

And when the dust settled, she went back to being her normal, absent self.

My mother needs help.

Mostly with getting sober and going through massive amounts of therapy, but we're absolutely broke and cannot afford any sort of private help. Never mind the fact that back when I had the energy to try and steer her in the direction of finding something free or working on it together, our conversations ended with her screaming at me for hours.

The sound of her voice echoes in my mind even now as I think about it, and I tug at my earlobes at the reminder.

I can't wait to turn eighteen and get out of here.

My phone vibrates again, but instead of a message with hope for the future, it's a reminder of my current responsibilities—Daphne is in the parking lot ready to chauffeur me to Books & Beans.

Lucas has practice, and although he offered to drive me after, I can't continually show up two hours past the start of my shift when Aunt Marie is manning the helm by herself.

"I have to head out," I tell Ms. Molinaro.

"Oh?"

"I'm closing at the store tonight."

"Of course, of course," she says, standing up to wave me out. "You have a good night, and tell Marie I said hello."

"Will do," I promise, turning back one final time. "And, seriously, I really appreciate your help."

She winks at me. "You got it."

Moments later, I climb into the backseat of Daphne's oversized SUV, and I'm off to feed, hydrate, and help entertain the fine people of this town.

I keep to myself as Zoe rambles on about some incident in her English class involving two theater students arguing over who deserved to read what part aloud. Her chatter is a nice soundtrack for the ride, giving me plenty of time to stare out the window and watch the mix of trees, buildings, and other cars zooming by us.

The shop is pretty busy when I arrive, so Daphne takes a rain check on the dessert I promised as a thank you, and she and Zoe head off for whatever their plans are.

I don my apron as I cross the tile, and in no time at all, I'm clocked in and enveloped in the well-established rhythm of taking orders, making drinks, ringing up books, making recommendations, and heating up food.

When I first started working at Books & Beans at age sixteen, I found it very overwhelming to multitask at this level—especially with the croaking sound of the steamer, the chatter of customers, and the bustle of everything else —but now, I find it kind of comforting. I'm able to keep a running mental to-do list, adding to it in tandem with clearing things off.

It makes the time pass fairly quickly, until finally, after what feels like hours of nonstop movement, everyone in the shop has been attended to or is sitting happily at a table with their purchases.

"That rush was unexpected," I say, letting out a breath.

"Good for business," Aunt Marie says as she dries her hands. "But bad for breaking in my new pair of Docs."

I laugh as I follow her gaze to her footwear. "They look cool, though."

"I know." She grins as she shows them off. "But I'm wearing three pairs of socks, and I can *still* feel the blisters forming."

Aunt Marie is about as different from my mother—her little sister—as she can be. Not only is she an accomplished businesswoman and functioning adult but her style is totally badass.

She recently dyed her naturally light blonde hair jet-black, which she said was the result of Saturday night boredom and a bottle of wine with her friends, and the drastic change works.

I mean, she's always been effortlessly chic, able to pull off different looks of overalls, bright purple lipstick, and floor-length velvet dresses.

And the tattoos on her arms are pure art.

I rub my fingers over my unblemished skin, shivering at the thought of needles permanently marking it.

In my life, when it comes to ink, I'm the odd woman out. Daphne and Zoe got matching hearts on their pinkies last summer after they both turned eighteen, and both of Aunt Marie's arms are covered in words, flowers, and artfully drawn mermaids.

I wonder if Lucas has any tattoos or if he wants any—maybe something to commemorate the sport he loves so much or whatever else in the world he likes.

Aunt Marie wipes down the nozzle on the steamer. "You want to take your break?"

"I'm good for now," I tell her. "Why don't you give those new shoes a rest?"

"Thank you." She sighs in relief. "I'm starving, too. Jessica had to head out early, so I've been on my own for longer than usual."

"Go," I encourage with a wave.

And she does.

In her absence, there's a steady after-work crowd, a stream of people stopping by to take some pastries to-go or to settle in and take advantage of the free internet.

But in between customers, I scan the new application I need to submit to fund my life post-graduation. It's pretty straightforward, and Ms. Molinaro was right about the changes to a preexisting essay, which will make things easier.

I slide my phone in my back pocket as the door chimes again, but instead of a stranger wearing a slightly wrinkled pantsuit or accompanied by a fussy child, I look up to find Lucas in a pair of joggers and a hoodie.

There's something about the way the fabric hits his shoulders and waist that I find immensely attractive.

I might be inexperienced, but I am human.

I feel the muscles of my mouth pull into a smile as he approaches, and he gives me one of his in return, revealing that dimple on his left side that causes my heart to skip a beat.

He steps up to the counter with his hands in his pockets. "Hey."

"What are you doing here?" I ask, leaning into my surprise instead of what else I'm feeling.

"Can't a guy come visit his girlfriend at work?" Lucas teases.

I chuckle. "Of course. But the gesture is kind of pointless, given no one we know is around."

He shrugs as he surveys the drink options, squinting at the list of names that are more complicated than what he drinks every morning. "What's good here?"

"Everything," I reply automatically.

"Good answer," he says with a smirk. "Employee of the month material, really."

"Uh-huh."

"Can you recommend something food-wise?" Lucas clarifies. "I think if I drink coffee now, I'll be up all night."

"The BLT's a classic." I tap on the glass of the display case. "And the chocolate peanut butter cookie with Reese's Pieces is really good. Those two items are probably my favorite."

"I'll take them both, please."

"Good choice."

I shuffle around to ready a plate for him, and he gives me a nod of appreciation as he watches me move.

"Seriously, why are you here?" I ask curiously. "Don't you have something better to do with your time?"

"Blunt and to the point as always, Kate." Lucas laughs dryly as he rubs the back of his neck. "I thought I'd come in and get another photo to post."

"Need my infinite wisdom on how to get the perfect picture?"

He shakes his head. "I think I've got this one, actually. Quick snap. Geolocation. Done."

I arrange his food neatly, then slide the plate across the counter. "If you're sure…"

"I am on that front, but I could use a book recommendation," Lucas muses, eyeing the nearest shelf. "I've been told I might like reading if I found the right book."

"I can help with that." I step around the counter. "How long are you planning on sticking around?"

"What time is your shift over?"

"Not for a few hours. I'm closing."

"I can hang out and give you a ride home," Lucas offers, then bites the corner of his mouth.

I lift my brows in surprise as I come to a stop in front of the bookshelf displaying our staff favorites. "You want to do that?"

"Yeah, it'll be nice."

"I…for what?" I manage through my confusion.

Lucas taps his knuckles on the spine of a random title. "As a gesture. You know, like in romance books."

"As much as I appreciate the offer, it's not exactly plot-worthy."

"Good thing you're here to help me pick a good story,

then," Lucas says confidently. "Show me the ways of a romantic."

I let out a breath, slightly daunted by the task. "Okay."

My eyes roam over the titles as I consider everything from high fantasy to Manga, even reading a few of the descriptions to get a refresher of the plot.

I'm looking for something that's the perfect mix of action and swoony, romantic storyline, but I come up short.

I give up on that quest somewhat quickly, instead stepping over to the wall of genre romance, wondering what would be an enjoyable example of the genre for him.

Something modern, for sure, maybe written in a first-person point of—

"Does it usually take this long to pick one?" Lucas asks in genuine curiosity.

"I'm feeling pressure to win you over," I admit.

He gives me a gentle smile. "If I don't like it, I'll just try another."

That answer makes me a little impulsive, and I grab something I don't normally recommend without caveats.

"Here," I say, handing him a copy of *My Alien King*.

I'm already on the third book of the series, so I know what he's in for, but if the cover gives him pause, he doesn't show it.

He simply accepts my recommendation without question.

And I like that trust.

Even if it's misplaced on his end.

I step back behind the counter to ring it up, along with his food items, giving him the employee discount that I've been a little too generous with lately.

"Thank you." He swipes his credit card, then tucks the book under his arm. "I'll let you know my thoughts."

I can't help but smirk. "Looking forward to it."

I don't get the pleasure of watching his retreat because another customer comes in—a frazzled mom looking for picture book recommendations—and I quickly move to assist her. It takes me far less time to put a stack in her very eager hands, and she leaves happy.

My aunt rejoins me shortly after that, thanking me for the time off her feet, and although we're still a while away from closing, she gets started on prepping and reorganizing for tomorrow.

I help her on and off as I work the register, alternating those duties with wiping down the nearest tables, but I'm conscious of Lucas's presence with each step I take.

And very aware that he's here because of me.

"Who's the guy?" Aunt Marie asks in a low voice.

I stop separating the garbage from the recycling. "What guy?"

She purses her lips as she tilts her head. "The one reading that very delicious book who keeps glancing up at you."

I follow her gaze, my eyes landing on Lucas at the same time he looks up to meet mine.

My face heats when my blush spreads. "That's Lucas Hunt. He's, uh, we go to school together."

He smiles at me as he pulls out his phone to take a picture of his book, the half-eaten cookie, and the Books & Beans napkin holder—further documentation of our relationship to post.

"Interesting," she says on a low chuckle.

"What is?" I ask, desperate for her take, even though she knows none of the details.

"Well," she says, leaning against the counter. "I've never seen a teenage boy so enthusiastic about reading a steamy romance in public on a night when my very fidgety niece is staying late."

I make a noncommittal noise as I straighten up a row of cup sleeves in their container.

But her tiny observation sticks with me through the rest of the shift.

EIGHT

"So, you're dating Lucas Hunt?"

Despite Zoe and Daphne's regular chatter and updates about the club over the past four years, I wasn't really sure what to expect when I joined the Rainbow Alliance.

Actually, that's not true.

I *thought* the meeting would be focused on upcoming actions, new initiatives, and planning for prom, but we only spent about the first five minutes on all that before the room turned into crafting chaos.

I suppose it's my own fault for joining so late in the game—graduation is less than two months away—because the only thing left to pull off is the big year-end photo area of prom. The club has been planning it all year, so after Daphne runs through the status of where everything is at, people just kind of hang out and decorate signs.

And gossip.

I wish we had more RA-related business to discuss, but I can't think of one single clarification I could possibly need about my assigned job as general helper in setting up for the dance.

I'm also learning that I'm the world's slowest painter, and although my mind can be creative at times, my physical body is not.

Compared to the other works of art coming to life with glitter and drawings and color, my blobs of black paint on the white poster are embarrassing.

No one calls me on it, though, focusing on their own projects and social groups.

All twenty desks in the room are full, but I'm mostly focused on my own cluster of four. One chair is occupied by Zoe, another by Austin—who's also in my Calculus class—and to my left sits a freshman named Miles, who is very interested in the details of my relationship.

"She totally is dating Lucas Hunt," Zoe answers proudly on my behalf.

Miles props his elbow on the desk as he angles his body toward me like we're about to exchange some deep dark secrets. "Tell. Me. Everything."

I press my back against the hard frame of my chair. "There's not really much to tell."

"It's *very* new," Zoe inserts with a wide smile.

"I figured," Miles admits. "But it's everywhere now. People want to know the details."

"People?" I breathe.

Zoe tucks her hair behind her ears as she leans in. "He rescued her on the side of the road after her car broke down, and he just fell for her right there."

"It's like a romcom come to life," Miles says with a happy sigh.

"I wouldn't go that far," I hedge.

"How far would you go, then?" Zoe asks, tone too mocking for my taste.

I level my gaze on her before I meet Miles's eyes. "We're just two normal people who like each other and want to date without falling into any clichés. You know? Just...like everyone else, I guess."

The words are so stilted coming out of my mouth, I internally cringe.

Lucas is much better at this kind of stuff, and I'm embarrassingly out of practice.

Not that I've ever really been *in* practice...

Zoe rolls her eyes. "Don't ruin this for me, Kate. My own best friend is the talk of the school right now."

I groan, even though that was precisely the goal.

Austin purses their lips and shakes their head. "If Kate doesn't want to talk about her super-hot boyfriend, she shouldn't have to."

"Thank you," I return, gesturing to them gratefully. "I agree."

"The less you talk, the more other people are going to do it for you," Miles points out.

I press my lips together, considering that.

"I mean, that whole thigh picture was..." He makes a chef-kiss motion. "Perfection."

"Miles," Austin says in a warning tone.

"Austin's right," Zoe grumbles reluctantly. "We don't want to scare Kate away from her first RA meeting. After all, she's missing a riveting afternoon of watching her boyfriend jog around in the spring sunshine, so I suppose we can cut her a little slack."

Miles sits up, eyes brightening. "Wait a second."

He hasn't even suggested anything yet, but I already don't like where his mind is going.

"Do you think he could get the baseball team to help hang posters?" Miles asks. "It would help us drive attention."

"I thought we *weren't* trying to scare her away," Austin mutters.

"I mean, it'd be huge," Miles continues. "Maybe he could share our posts on his account to let people know it's happening? And get them to help?"

I grimace as I mentally run through the calendar.

Because not only do I not want to volunteer him for something without his permission, I don't even know if we'll still be fake-dating then.

I sigh and fiddle with the strap on my bag. "No promises. But I'll ask him."

"Good." Zoe beams at me before she gives Miles a conspiratorial look. "Did you hear about the plans for spring break yet? We're thinking of..."

I pull myself out of the conversation before she even finishes her sentence.

I get that Lucas wanted me to join a club to get more visibility for our "relationship," but I'm not sure this is helping anything other than placating the whims of a nosy freshman.

Obviously it's a good thing for me to be involved and support my two best friends and the goal of the RA, but I'd rather be slinging coffees and recommending books and contributing to my savings account.

"Knock-knock."

I jerk up at the sound of Lucas's voice, which is paired almost instantly with Miles's unintelligible screech.

I don't blame him, honestly.

Even I can't deny the allure of the sight of Lucas in a backward hat and his gray—of *course* they're gray—sweatpants and tight-fitting shirt.

"Can I come in?" Lucas asks no one in particular.

"Yes!" Zoe says, waving him over.

He crosses the room, unbothered by all the people gawking at him as he comes to stand behind my chair.

Even worse, he drapes his arms down over my shoulders and across my chest to give me kind of an odd hug from behind that assaults my senses with spearmint.

It's been, like, two hours since I've seen him last, and I don't know if I'm supposed to do something to greet him or show affection.

But I'm unable to do anything other than fidget until he releases me.

"Daniel Fullerton and Lucas Hunt in our little rainbow meeting?" Zoe says, rubbing her hands together in excitement. "What a day."

I was so focused on Lucas that I didn't even notice his teammate trailing behind him.

"You're welcome!" Daniel says, speaking a little louder than necessary.

Lucas laughs good-naturedly. "It's an honor, really. Am I interrupting?"

"No." I shake my head as I drop my brush. "I mean, yes, kind of. But, uh, I'm glad to see you."

"I like to hear that," he says before he eyes the poster in front of me.

"And now that we're here," Daniel says, slinging an arm around Lucas's shoulder, "is it too late in the year to join?"

"Of course not," Daphne says, leaving her seat behind to address his question. "But you have practice."

"I'm flattered that you know my schedule," Daniel says, beaming.

Lucas rolls his eyes and shoves his friend away. "But we can go to stuff outside of meetings or help with whatever you need."

I know he's just saying this to keep up our cover, so I feel bad at how excited the other members of the RA seem to be getting at the increased attention.

And, of course, I can't forget the promise I made to them just a few minutes ago.

"Can you help spread the word about the RA photo booth at prom?" I ask Lucas. "I think we'll be hanging up these posters when they're dried next week."

"For sure," he answers without hesitation.

"And if you could help us out the day of, too," Miles pipes up. "That'd be fantastic."

But now, my guilt at ambushing him momentarily overcomes the *other* guilt I feel over this whole situation, and we haven't nailed down the details yet.

"Are you sure?" I add, giving him an out. "I mean, we still haven't made plans, and it's a little while away…"

Lucas ignores or doesn't pick up on my signal emphasizing the time frame. "I'm in."

"Me, too," Daniel adds.

"Fantastic," Miles squeals in elation. "It's going to be great to spread awareness of our group. And create long-lasting memories of the night. Well, for you. I'm not invited."

There's an awkward pause where everyone's just looking at Miles with pity, and I clear my throat.

"So, uh, what's going on?" I ask our visitors. "Did practice let out early?"

Lucas nods. "Since we have the game tomorrow, we kept it light today. And I thought I'd swing by and see if you need a ride."

"I'm not finished with this yet," I say, tapping the edge of my poster.

"We'll finish up for you," Zoe says. "Everyone else is almost done."

Lucas quirks a brow at me. "I don't mind waiting, though."

Zoe is bouncing in her chair, watching our interaction, and I'm eager to escape her scrutiny and call it quits on today.

"Do you mind?" I ask him. "You don't have other plans?"

"What's more important than spending more time with my girlfriend?" Lucas picks my bag up from the floor and slings it over his shoulder. "Can't say no to that."

I withhold a huff at his smugness as I stand up beside him.

"Well, we'll see you later," Daphne says. "We're grateful for the extra help and any promotion, of course."

"Anytime," Lucas says, pressing a hand to my back as we start to walk.

"And I'll take over on this," Daniel says, jumping for the chair I just vacated. "Hey, I'm Daniel."

Austin rolls their eyes. "I know. We're in the same English class."

"Are we?" Daniel acts affronted. "And you've never said hello?"

I lose track of the conversation as Lucas and I walk quickly through the halls.

We walk at a pace that makes me feel like we've just escaped getting caught robbing a bank when all we did was volunteer our time and talk to a very chatty group of people.

It's easy for him, I think, to be *on* all the time, but I definitely appreciate the silence as we settle into his car.

After I buckle in, I run through a few sets of deep breaths. Unwinding from social situations is usually something I do on my own, but I don't mind going through my exercises as Lucas drives and the whoosh of fresh air comes through the cracked window.

In fact, now that I think about it, all this week, Lucas has refrained from listening to music while we drive. I don't know if that's because he knows I'm sensitive to the sound or if he just wants to talk, but before I can ask about it, he opens his mouth.

"You know, you didn't tell me I was reading alien porn."

His sentence hits me, and for a beat, I'm stunned.

And then a genuine laugh escapes me.

I'm so taken aback by his casual statement that waves of chuckles roll through me, and I find no reason to suppress them.

Because it is *funny*.

It takes a full minute for it to peter out, and it's only

because I catch Lucas's smirk of amusement that I come back to normal.

"So, you got to chapter seven, then?" I ask knowingly. "The one with the—"

"I found the alternative use for a spatula entertaining to say the least."

"Well, imagine if you were from an alien planet and there were just all these gadgets around," I tease. "Items you've never come across...although, thinking it through, it's a little odd that he has no idea what a whisk is, given that his people fly in spaceships and have guns with laser beams in them."

"I guess these things aren't made to be read for the believability factor," Lucas poses, glancing at me as we idle at a stoplight.

"No. Not really." I'm sure he sees the redness on my cheeks, but I don't care. "So, you liked it, then?"

"It's not bad."

He and I both break out into a round of laughter at that admission.

"Not the best but not the worst," I admit.

"Agreed." Lucas scratches the back of his neck. "So, uh, am I supposed to be taking you to Books & Beans? Or home? Or did you want to go somewhere else for a bit?"

I shake my head. "Home, please."

Lucas refocuses on the road as the light turns green. "Can do. You know, when you mentioned this morning you had to switch shifts, I couldn't help but think how convenient it was that you won't be able to make it to my game tomorrow..."

I tug the ends of my hair. "I know. And you probably

don't believe me, but I didn't plan that. It was part of the compromise for getting coverage for today with the new girl, and I already told Zoe and Daphne that I'd join—"

"It's okay, Kate." He taps on the steering wheel with his palms. "I'm not mad or disappointed or whatever. I'm just giving you a hard time. Joking around."

"Oh."

I don't know what else to say, so I lower the window a little more, pressing my fingers against the pressure of the spring air flying by.

"But I was looking forward to seeing you in the stands," Lucas says after a moment.

"Really?"

"All my teammates will have their families and who they're dating there. And some people go all out...you know, dressing up in school colors and decorating our lockers and stuff."

I quirk a brow. "Did Sydney use to do that for you?"

"Well, yeah."

"Right." For some reason, I feel all irritated inside at the comparison. "I'm not exactly the most crafty or the most school-spirited, so I'm not sure I'm up for all that."

"You don't have to be," Lucas assures me. "But it wouldn't hurt if you wore a shirt with our school name on it or something tomorrow."

It takes me all of three seconds to catalog my wardrobe in my drawers at home, and the closest thing I have to any sort of branded clothing is for Books & Beans.

"I don't have anything like that," I say with a frown.

"We'll have to fix that," he says resolutely.

My mind is still stuck on Sydney, imagining her showing up in a full-blown cheerleading uniform—although, I don't think that's a thing in baseball—and wowing the crowd with her knowledge of the sport and her pride in being with Lucas.

I wipe my palms on the holey old jeans I got from Zoe. "Have you had any run-ins?"

Lucas glances at me. "What?"

"With Sydney," I clarify. "Has she called you or come over or whatever?"

"No," he answers, relaxing his posture. "Her friends have been stalking my posts, but I haven't heard anything from her directly. Thankfully."

"So, it's working, then?"

"I guess it is."

"Good."

Lucas takes off his hat to run his hands through his hair, then a look of realization crosses his features. "Here, take this."

I quirk a brow. "I'm not really a hat person."

"Until now." He keeps one eye on the road as he puts it on top of my head. "Perfect."

I appraise myself in the side-view mirror, adjusting it accordingly. "Not bad."

"You're playing your part well," he tells me. "I know I still have to hold up my end of the bargain. Not all the parts have arrived yet. I started dismantling your transmission only to find a problem with one of the belts, which then led me to another issue entirely..."

I wince. "Sounds expensive."

"Not really," Lucas says as we turn down my street.

"Parts are parts. It's the labor that's expensive. But *I* am free."

"At the cost of my pristine reputation," I deadpan.

"If that's all you're trading in, I think you're getting the better end of the deal."

I roll my eyes as I remove his hat and fluff my hair. "Says the guy whose ex-girlfriend is no longer stalking him."

"Well, I have been busy. Harder to track down. You know, being actively in-season *and* having a girlfriend *and* keeping up with the hunters from planet Eckdor *and* getting an offer to join the Rainbow Alliance..."

"If it's too much, you can just text me next time instead of showing up," I retort.

"But then I wouldn't have gotten to see you one last time today," Lucas says without a shred of teasing or humor in his tone.

I nearly whimper at that line.

I get that it's good practice to flirt and banter when we're alone so we don't bungle it when other people are around, but his words stop me short.

If I let them have their true power and effect on me, the results could be devastating.

So, I swallow the elation and butterflies as we come to a stop in front of my house.

"You don't have to say stuff like that when it's just us, you know," I murmur.

He shrugs as he turns toward me, then squints as he looks just past my shoulder. "Hey, is your front door open?"

I turn to see that, yes, it is open, blowing gently in the wind, and my stomach drops.

"I'll take care of it."

Lucas moves his hand to undo his seatbelt. "Maybe I should go and check it—"

"No," I say sharply. "It's fine."

"Are you sure? I don't mind coming in."

"I've got it."

And to emphasize my point, I hurriedly grab my belongings.

"Kate, I can—"

"I'll see you tomorrow," I interrupt as I jump out. "Thanks for the ride. Seriously. And the hat."

I practically sprint up the front walk before he can change his mind and follow me.

And just to prove—to myself, I think—that I don't need him, I slam the door shut and lock it behind me, not daring to move until I hear him pull away.

He does so after a minute, with the music turned up and the engine roaring, and I let out a breath.

With dread and trepidation swirling in my chest, I move further inside toward the kitchen, stepping over the warped and slightly charred cookie sheets that someone tossed aside.

The cabinets are all open, and they've clearly been ransacked. Along with the dishware, most of the food has been cleaned out.

I quickly do my best to get the place back in order, putting our minimal belongings in their places.

Unfortunately, I'm used to this cleanup process.

This is something that happens far too often, and it's

one of the reasons why I installed a lock on my bedroom door. The hardware was pricey and a little complex to put in, but the added security is proving to be necessary.

I move through the kitchen and stop to pick up a packet of noodles. It's chicken flavor, which is my favorite. We usually run out very quickly and I barely got any the last two times I shopped, so I hid a package in my room last time I went to the store.

But unless my mom has been out shopping on her own…

I dash down the hallway and cry out at the sight of the giant hole at the bottom of my bedroom door. The new lock held up, but the flimsy wood has been kicked in.

My hands shake as I properly unlock it to assess the damage to my room, and when I step in, I find that it's worse than I thought.

My bookshelf has been nearly cleared out, its contents likely to be sold off to some secondhand store, and the minimal makeup products I've amassed are gone.

At least my clothes seem to be untouched—they wouldn't earn anything on consignment, anyway—so that's one less thing I have to worry about.

Still, I feel violated that someone has done this and that it's likely my mother *let* it happen to make a quick buck.

That even after how hard I've worked and how careful I am, I still have no control over what happens to me or my home.

And so with the sharp prick of tears in my eyes, I lie down on my mattress in defeat.

NINE

My life has been rinse and repeat for nearly two weeks.

It's full of shifts at Books & Beans, homework, tweaking my grant essay, and Lucas.

Holding his hand is so normal now that I don't hesitate to initiate contact with him in the hallways; although, I'm still *very* aware of his presence and the feel of our fingers entwined.

We've actually gotten pretty good at existing in the same place—he'll occasionally join me for lunch in the library as a silent companion and visit me at Books & Beans after practice—and he's on top of the whole vague photo thing for his feeds.

I've even swallowed my pride and faced boredom and made it to *three* of his practices. I spent most of the time reading instead of watching him move around the field, but he seemed satisfied enough with my attendance.

He's also been texting me pictures of the progress he's made on my car. It kind of just looks like a mess of parts and grease-stained rags, but he assures me things are moving forward.

As far as fake boyfriends go, I suppose he isn't the worst.

"You okay?" Lucas asks suddenly.

We've been walking in sync through the science wing, but he pulls me to the side of the hall before I can step into my AP Chem classroom.

I blink at the quick movement. "Yeah."

His gaze of interest—or concern, maybe—doesn't falter. "You sure?"

I furrow my brows. "Sorry, did I miss something?"

"You just seemed a little lost in thought. More than usual, I guess."

"I was," I admit with a smile. "I was thinking about you."

His eyebrows shoot up at my admission. "Really? What about?"

"That you're pretty okay to be around. Tolerable most of the time. Especially when you're silent."

He chuckles as he takes a step closer. "High praise, coming from you."

"The compliments are scarce, but I say what I mean," I tell him.

"You're nothing if not honest, Kate," Lucas says, raising a hand.

I think he's going to run his long fingers through his hair, but instead, I watch wordlessly as they move closer to my face.

I back up slightly, leaning against the wall as he traces a

line down my cheek, and I have to fight the flutter of my eyelids so they don't give away how nice this feels.

"Especially when it comes to which book of the *Alien King* series is the best," he finishes.

I let out a laugh, willing the humor to break through the cord of tension in my body. "You haven't even read the sixth one yet. There's this scene where—"

"There are six of those books?" Lucas sputters as he drops his hand.

"Ten," I correct.

He groans. "*Ten?*"

"If you keep up your current pace, you can finish them by graduation for sure."

"My new goal," Lucas says resolutely. "We're accomplishing a lot together already."

"I suppose so."

A pointed clearing of a throat catches both of our attention, and in my fear that a teacher has come to reprimand us—for what, I'm not sure—I straighten up.

But it's only Sydney and her friends, shooting us looks of disapproval as they walk by.

"Some people are so gross with their PDA," one of them scoffs. "I mean, come on. It's a public hallway. Like, so gross."

"Definitely not as romantic as that date he took you on for your birthday last year," the other friend supplies with a mischievous glint in her eye.

Sydney and I lock gazes for only a nanosecond, but I feel the tremendous weight of it.

"Come on," she mutters to her entourage.

I hold myself stoically until they've crossed the threshold and are out of earshot.

Aside from a few glares and some staring, I haven't had to deal with any negative fallout from this situation. I've read enough books where there's a horrible conflict just for the sake of it, and I'm really not trying to perpetuate negative stereotypes for other women.

Thankfully, it seems like Sydney is going to be a nonissue for me.

"She planned it," Lucas says quietly.

I feel my brows pull together. "What?"

"Sydney planned this elaborate birthday date for herself," he explains. "Said that what I wanted to do wasn't 'enough' for her."

"What were you going to do?" I ask before I can overthink why I'm so curious for the answer.

"I booked a reservation at some fancy restaurant she'd been dropping hints about for months and got her concert tickets to see her favorite singer. Even though I can't *stand* any of her songs. But I was going to make a big night of it and everything."

"That's...nice. I guess."

He snorts. "You wouldn't like that, though."

I tilt my head as our eyes meet. "You're so certain?"

"I am. Because you don't like loud music. Or crowds. And you don't seem to have a taste for things like overpriced filets of salmon or ice cream made from brie and pears."

"No," I say slowly. "I don't."

"In fact, I think if you really got your way for a whole day, you'd rather spend it alone than with someone else. But I'm sure I can come up with something."

"Like what?"

"When's your birthday?" Lucas asks instead, pulling out his phone.

"Beginning of May."

"What day?"

"The sixth."

He smiles as he marks it on his calendar. "Well, I suppose you'll just have to wait and find out, then."

I swallow.

It's a little cruel to think about, given that we'll be broken up by then, and it will be one of the mysteries of life I'll never uncover.

I suppose I can live with that.

Or I'll just have to cope.

The bell rings, chiming loudly through the speaker on the ceiling above our heads.

I smile tightly at him, then turn away. "You're going to be late for class."

"Wait," Lucas says.

When I spin back, he hands over my bag.

"Oh, thanks. I almost forgot about that."

"I've got you."

And then he moves quickly, zigzagging to the side to press a quick kiss to my lips. "See you later, Kate."

I don't move after he heads off because I'm startled into stagnation by the gesture.

The feeling of his lips on mine was so brief but also so...everything.

I'm not too embarrassed to admit that I've visualized

what it would be like to be kissed, and I've read enough steamy romance novels to recognize the signs of fluttering in my body.

My feet move forward, but my body is floating up on a cloud as I find my seat in the room.

I replay the kiss over and over in my mind, trying to remember just how it felt, and I barely register the instructions for today's lab. Something about a page of notes to follow and an advanced experiment that's a little dangerous...

"Kate?"

I pinch my eyes shut, then open them and force myself to smile at my teacher. "Yes, Mr. Oria?"

"Go ahead and join Sydney at her table." His tone makes it clear it's not the first time he's requested I do this. "Now."

I glance to the spot next to me in horror, realizing that my normal lab partner is out today, and the only vacant spot is beside Sydney.

At the very least, as I shuffle within the bounds of her overly sweet perfume, our proximity kills every lingering lusty feeling I have toward Lucas—especially when I consider how many times they did something like that and who knows what else.

That thought actually makes me feel a little nauseated.

As a distraction, I decide to throw everything I can into our little experiment today.

The goal is to create an exothermic reaction by mixing aluminum and iodine, and although I prefer the arts over the sciences, I'm able to force my brain to focus on grinding the iodine beads into powder and moving through the rest of the steps.

It's kind of nice to get lost in my concentration the same way I do with a good book.

Sydney and I are the first pair to finish our prep, so I take small careful steps as I carry our plate over to the fume hood, which is a square box that will vent out any toxins through a filtration system.

"I'll add the water," Sydney offers.

I nod, even though that is definitely the simplest and most rewarding part, according to our textbook.

Once I've got the setup ready, she squirts a few drops on top of the little pyramid of powder, then pulls her hand out as the mixture starts bubbling.

That's all that happens at first, then suddenly, there's a spark and a cloud of purple smoke, like the beginnings of a volcanic eruption.

"Class!" Mr. Oria calls. "Come over and see."

Everyone excitedly abandons their workstations to come watch as our experiment continues smoking—which is all sucked up by the machine—and then catches fire.

The effect elicits a gasp and a jump from Sydney, whose face reddens in embarrassment.

"Sorry," she says, tucking her long blonde hair behind her ears.

Some people pull out their phones to record the action, including Mr. Oria, and I do the same because Lucas has gotten me in the habit of documenting things.

I adjust the phone to catch a good angle of the smoke and fire, then send it off to him.

I don't expect him to answer, given that he's likely slogging through his Calculus class on the other side of the school, but his reply is instant.

Should I call the fire department?

I smile. *No need. Just celebrating a successful exothermic reaction.*

I'm not even going to ask what that means. You're too smart for me, Kate.

I roll my eyes at his teasing and move to put my phone away, but another text comes through from him.

I was thinking…are you free this weekend?

Lucas was thinking about me?

I suppose that isn't a new or riveting concept, but…

I bite my lip as a third little blue bubble appears from him.

You could come over on Saturday, and I'll show you the progress of your car. If you're up for it?

I can't on Saturday.

Oh.

Working a double at B&B.

He sends me a frowning face. *Okay.*

My fingers fly over the keys. *I'm free Sunday morning, though.*

It's a date.

And stupid, stupid me is in a good mood for the rest of the period.

I can't think of a time when I would ever describe my mood as "giggly," but that's the feeling I hold inside my chest, even as Sydney and I get roped into taking on the majority of cleaning up after everyone and disposing of materials so other students can use the fume hood.

When the bell rings, I carefully wash and dry my hands

as my classmates dissipate, and just as I move to put my safety glasses back in the cabinet, Sydney steps up beside me.

"Oh, hey," I say nonchalantly.

"I'm in love with him," she blurts, uncaring that there are still people within earshot.

I'm sure that will go over super well for the gossip circuit.

"I'm *still* in love with him," Sydney amends.

Of course, I immediately know who she's talking about.

But I'm at a total loss for how to respond.

I mean, I knew that she and Lucas were serious and together for a while, but *love*?

"I'm, uh, sorry?" I sputter.

Her eyes drop down to my scuffed-up sneakers before she meets my eyes again. "No. You're not."

I swallow and shift on my feet. "I mean, kind of. I don't like seeing other people in pain."

As I say it, I realize that's exactly what I recognize in her.

And while I am happy to go along with this fake relationship for my gain, I guess I never considered the fallout for everyone else.

Namely, her.

Because I'm on Team Lucas, hearing about their relationship and breakup from his end, not thinking about how much she's probably hurting.

Sydney smiles, but it's flat and doesn't meet her eyes. "I just...I don't even know why I'm talking to you about this."

I grimace as I wring my hands. "I don't either."

She sighs and flips her hair over her shoulder. "Listen,

it's hard seeing you two together. Like, I thought this year was going to be so different. Valentine's day carnations. Spring break trip. Prom. But without Lucas, nothing on my senior year vision board has come to fruition."

In some ways, I'm relieved to be confronted by her honesty instead of some catty behavior inspired by *Mean Girls*, but I'm also uncertain if this is some sort of weird psychological warfare that I'm not equipped to handle.

"I should get going," I say, stepping around her. "I'll…"

I don't even know how to finish that sentence, so I simply grab my bag and get the hell out of there.

TEN

Aunt Marie agreed to drop me off at Lucas's house on the way to work this morning.

It's early for a Sunday by most people's standards, and it feels like the entire neighborhood we're driving through is still asleep, but it's a normal hour for two people who work at a coffee shop.

"It's right up ahead," she murmurs, eyes flicking between the navigation app on her phone and the numbers on the houses.

"Yeah," I confirm with a nod. "I think it's this one. With the red brick."

She lets out a low whistle as she comes to a stop.

This place isn't particularly fancy, but it's still a far cry from what she and I are accustomed to.

That reaction aside, she's been relatively chill about the whole thing with Lucas—or rather, she hasn't pried for any details about the guy who's shown up for almost all my shifts lately.

I wasn't planning on introducing them because I didn't see the point, but I came out of the stockroom last week with a stack of cups to find the two of them chatting happily at the counter.

And now, every time I mention Lucas, which I don't think is *too* often, she gives me a wide smile of amusement.

"Will you need me to come pick you up?" Aunt Marie asks as I unbuckle.

I shake my head. "I think I'll be set. But thank you. Seriously. I owe you."

"You don't owe me at all, Kate," she says sternly. "Just focus on having fun."

"You, too," I say as I step out.

She smiles at me before she pulls away, leaving me standing in front of Lucas's house, clutching my bag against my chest.

I should have brought flowers or baked goods or something because I suddenly feel a little silly just showing up on his doorstep with my tattered bag at eight o'clock—and I feel even more out of place as I approach.

The house is modest but well kept, and even only judging by the front facade, it feels like a *home*. The flowerbeds have already been prepared for spring, and a sign for Lucas's baseball team hangs in the window.

The closest my own mother has come to supportive decor was when she taped my first pay stub to the front of the fridge—because she mistakenly took it for a valid check and didn't want to forget to cash it.

I sigh as I step onto the cement path that leads from the driveway to the front door, tapping the side of Lucas's car for good luck.

When I reach the door, I knock, rapping my knuckles against the wood three times, and count the seconds until it opens.

The woman with the same blue eyes as Lucas greets me with a smile. "Kate! Hi."

I plaster on my most pleasant customer service grin. "Hello."

"I'm Lauren, Lucas's mother," she says brightly. "It's so nice to meet you."

"You, too."

"Come in," she says, inviting me in with a wave.

"Thank you. I know it's a bit early…" I tuck my hair behind my ears as I scope out the interior. "But, uh, you have a really nice house."

"That's sweet of you to say." Lauren leads me through a very beige but very clean sitting room. "I've recently done a little redecorating, so it's nice to hear my efforts are appreciated. Lord knows Lucas doesn't notice."

"Really?" I step through a rounded archway toward the kitchen where everything is painted a dark green. "He's usually pretty observant."

"With you, maybe," Lauren says lightly. "But I'm his mother, and he doesn't have the same appreciation for my interests."

I chuckle at that. "Lucas and I don't really have that much in common, actually."

I suppose it's a strange thing to admit to my supposed boyfriend's mother, but she lets out a howl of laughter.

"So, you're telling me that he's been reading a bunch of alien erotica books all on his own?"

The minimal confidence I've accumulated while navigating this conversation implodes, and I'm left stunned into silence as I hover between the kitchen island and the counter.

I seriously debate turning around and hightailing it out of here.

"You should see your face right now," she wheezes, still emitting rumbles of laughter.

I don't even know what to do, so I stand somewhat stiffly as she pats my back.

I can feel the heat on my cheeks. "I, um…"

"Oh, Kate, I didn't mean to embarrass you." Her voice wobbles as she tries to shift back to her normal cadence. "I've been trying to get Lucas to enjoy reading for years, but when I came home one night and found him with *My Alien King*, I about died."

I wince. "Sorry."

"No, no, I think it's funny! Plus, I loved that series."

"Okay," I say uncertainly. "That's good."

She lets out a breath as she gazes around the room, like she's trying to remember herself. "Well, Lucas is already out back. Do you want something to drink?"

I'm not about to ask this woman for anything when I'm already feeling so off-kilter, but before I can say no, she reaches into the cabinet for a mug.

"I was just about to take a cup of coffee out to him. Would you like one?"

"That would…" I swallow the shredded remnants of my pride. "That would be great, actually. I'm dragging today."

"Late night?"

I shrug. "I opened and closed the store, and we had to do a bunch of prep for a catering order this afternoon."

"Lucas mentioned you work at that cute coffee shop across town." Lauren reaches for another mug. "The one with all the books?"

I nod, appreciating the extra-large size and the cool swirls on the cups. "My aunt owns it, so I've been making lattes forever."

"Oh, can you do the fun little designs with the foam?"

"Aunt Marie can," I tell her. "She's a master with that kind of stuff. Bakes most of the treats herself, too. I'm hopeless at it, but I compensate by being the best bookseller in the store."

"An entrepreneur," Lauren says appreciatively as she pours the coffee, then the milk.

"Just a normal book lover, I think."

"That works, too." She stirs in a mix of caramel and hazelnut syrup, then beams at her work. "There, I'll get the door for you."

"Thanks," I say, carefully picking up the mugs.

She opens the sliding glass door that leads from the kitchen to the back patio. "Let me know if you two need anything else. I was thinking of grabbing takeout for lunch."

I smile at her as best I can. "It was nice to meet you."

I hope I don't sound too dismissive, but the last thing I need is to hang around and make more of a fool out of myself in front of my pseudo-boyfriend's mother.

She smiles widely. "You, too."

I try to shake off the conversation by focusing on not spilling our precious beverages or stumbling over the stone path that trails through the grass toward what looks like a big barn.

As I get closer, I get the impression that this is Lucas's makeshift workshop. The sound of an old, scratchy radio carries over the air, and I can smell oil and other products I can't identify.

But, most notably, I see the way Lucas reacts at my arrival—eyes bright, dimple revealed, posture easy.

It's pure elation.

He kills the music as he jumps up. "Hey, let me help you."

"I'm in grave danger of giving myself a coffee bath, but I couldn't resist your mom's extra special brew, which I now know is just a ton of sugar and fancy artificial flavoring," I joke, overcompensating for my misinterpretation of his eagerness by babbling.

He wraps his fingers around the mug—and my hand—as he leans in to kiss me on the cheek.

"Can't deny that it's good, though," he says playfully.

I don't have any response because the place where his lips briefly touched is now on fire, and I fear I'll be able to focus on nothing but the burn for hours.

Apparently, it's just a totally normal thing between us that he *kisses* me now.

He's taken us to the next step without consulting me, and I'm not sure how to feel about it.

I mean, it was just the other day he gave me my first ever kiss—although, I don't think he knows that—and it was in the middle of the school hallway like the intimacy was no big deal.

I guess for him, with all his experience and charm and wiles, it's nothing.

But for me, it's everything.

And then some.

It shouldn't be, though, because this is just a temporary situation, and I got a dose of that reality when I was snapped out of the cloud by the AP Chem experiment.

Well, by the iodine, aluminum, and Sydney—who is, apparently, still in love with my fake boyfriend.

Which, now that I'm thinking about it, is equal parts devastating and infuriating.

I take a breath, gripping my mug in both hands as I settle on a stool beside my torn-apart car.

I don't know if it's my embarrassment with Lauren or the interaction with Sydney or the kissing with Lucas, but I'm suddenly feeling very overwhelmed and wishing I had my headphones to block everything out.

I mean, Lucas is just out here getting women to love him and prancing around with grease stains on his face and white t-shirt without a care in the world.

Even worse, he's *smiling* at me.

"Did you know that Sydney is still in love with you?" I blurt.

My question comes right after he's taken a sip, and he chokes even as his eyes widen at my words.

"What?" Lucas asks between coughs.

I wince at the sputtering I've caused, and the situation, then explain as calmly as I can.

"She and I ended up being partnered in AP Chem. You know that video I sent you? She helped. Well, kind of. Mostly, she swooped in at the end and took half the credit. But, uh, yeah, after the bell rang, she cornered me and told me that she's still in love with you."

He lets out a long sigh, pinching his eyes shut for a beat before he meets my gaze. "I'm sorry."

"Why?"

"She shouldn't have dragged you into it."

"I'm not worried about me."

I take a long sip, finding the drink just as delicious as it was the first time I tried it on the way to school. I should have had a cup of coffee before I arrived here—maybe that would have saved me from the humiliation in the kitchen and stopped me from dropping this bomb on Lucas.

"You shouldn't worry about her either, though," he insists. "Her feelings are a non-issue."

"That's pretty insensitive," I say sharply.

I don't know why I'm suddenly Sydney Smith's champion, but when I recall her sadness and vulnerability, I can't help it.

I'm the sucker who roots for the person the main character *doesn't* choose in a love triangle, which may or may not say a lot about how I would function in a real relationship.

Lucas narrows his eyes at me over the rim of his mug. "You don't know what happened. If you did, I don't think you'd be on her side."

I quirk a challenging brow. "Then tell me."

I'm almost certain he'll fire back, so I take another drink, needing to be fully caffeinated for the battle.

But he merely sighs as he takes the seat beside me. "It's complicated."

"Do you still...have feelings for her?" I press, feeling very much like Zoe at the moment.

"No." His single word is full of resolve, like there's no questioning it. "I definitely don't."

"Is that what happened, then? You didn't feel the same way she did?"

"That's part of it."

Lucas is being frustratingly coy, but I get it.

He's comfortable with the surface-level—by his standards—physical intimacy, but the emotional stuff isn't somewhere he wants to go.

It's not my place to force him, so I let him off the hook.

"Well, should we get started?" I suggest as I eye the big red movable tower of tools. "On second thought, that looks kind of intimidating."

"It's really not."

He smiles that Lucas-smile of his while watching me stand and peek into where the transmission once sat, which is now an empty hole.

I wrinkle my nose. "Maybe I'll just read while you do all these car things."

"Or we could talk?"

I perk up as he joins me, pressing his hands against the rusted side of my MR2 before he starts.

"My parents are getting a divorce. And it's all my fault."

Once again, I am speechless.

"Sydney and I were together for, like, three months before she wanted to have a big 'meet the families' dinner. Afterward, she was all excited because it was a big success and everyone got along great. We didn't find out until a few months later that her mom and my dad *really* hit it off."

Lucas pauses and taps the metal with both hands.

"I got home early from practice one day," he continues.

"My dad had thought the house would be empty because my mom was working late…"

I'm able to connect the dots, and I set my cup aside in favor of focusing on him.

He clears his throat. "Needless to say, my parents have been separated ever since. And my dad doesn't even seem to care. He packed up and moved in with Sydney's mom."

I want to comfort him, but I don't know how.

I decide to try to acknowledge the situation without making him feel like I pity him, which is what I would want if he ever found out about the stuff with my mom.

"That really sucks."

He lets out a low rumble of laughter. "It does."

"And now, Sydney's going to be your—"

"Don't say it," Lucas begs. "It'll be so much worse."

I frown. "So, you didn't break up because you don't have feelings for her, then? You broke up because you just, like, didn't want all that?"

"The whole thing with our parents was the final straw, but we were heading that direction anyway." He exhales through his nose. "To be honest, the only good thing to come out of the situation was the end of our relationship."

"But she thinks you broke up because of your parents? Not because you don't feel the same way?"

"I've told her. Many, many times. But she won't hear it." He looks down into the empty hole where my engine used to be before he meets my gaze. "That's why I had to take drastic measures."

I nod as I process this information, taking a step back to see the pain on his features juxtaposed against the mess of the garage.

And I use it as a way out of this intense conversation.

"You've certainly taken some here," I gesture around us before picking up a set of pliers. "I mean, these are pretty much torture devices."

He looks up, seeming surprised I don't want to hear more.

But he lets it go.

"Only you would think of that. Reading some serial killer book these days?"

"No," I scowl. "But I am reading the latest book in my favorite mafia romance series, and it's a little dark."

"I'll have to do that one next, then." He plucks the pliers from my hand, puts them away, and takes out a wrench instead. "If you recommend it, that is."

"I'll let you know if I think you'll like it," I reply, taking a seat once again to watch him work.

The natural soundtrack his movement provides is quite nice as he mills around the space and rifles for the right tools and tinkers with different parts, so I happily reach for my tablet and prop my feet up on his vacant seat.

"You know, I'm glad you're here," he says after a little while.

"Me, too." It's an easy admission. "Really glad."

He taps a wrench on his thigh as he mulls over whatever he's thinking. "You're not like anyone else I've ever met."

"Oh, god," I groan, tangling my fingers in my hair. "You can't tell me I have 'not like other girls' energy, Lucas."

"What's so bad about that? It's true."

Even if it is, I'm not sure how I feel about it.

Or any of this, really.

ELEVEN

"Has Lucas talked to you about spring break at all?" Zoe asks.

She normally speaks at a pretty rapid pace, but her question comes out at light speed.

I'm guessing it's because she knows we only have about twenty more steps until we split off—her and Daphne to the cafeteria, me to the library.

"No," I answer quickly.

We're exactly halfway through our estimated arrangement of fake dating, and so far, we've talked about a lot—more than I expected, actually—but out of everything we've waded into, his plans for next week haven't come up.

"Really?" Zoe balks, eyes wide in surprise.

I guess, as someone who is supposed to be falling more deeply in love with him as each day passes, that should be more of an issue.

I wince at my oversight. "I mean, it hasn't come up. He

knows I'm just working as many shifts as I can get all week, and he's probably got practices and stuff."

That, thankfully, I'll be too busy to attend.

"But he has the tournament," Zoe says.

"The what?"

She gives me a look like I'm the most exasperating human on the planet. "The baseball tournament."

"It's an annual thing up in Erie," Daphne supplies. "A bunch of teams around the state show up, and they play as many games as they can until they're knocked out."

"Can't say I'm sad about missing that," I mumble.

"It's actually kind of fun," Daphne tells me. "I tagged along to one of my brother's tournaments a few years ago, and trust me, the added pressure to win to stay in adds to the experience."

"Oh."

Zoe rolls her eyes. "But a bunch of people, *including* your best friend, will be tagging along for this one."

"What?" I balk. "Why are *you* going?"

"There's a waterpark up there," Daphne explains. "And since so many students are going, players from the team and their significant others, it's offering some big discount on the hotel and park access."

"That makes sense, I guess."

"Amanda Gorski invited us," Zoe adds. "And you should *totally* come."

"She has to work," Daphne repeats on my behalf.

"I do," I chime in. "Many, many hours."

"Well, you could talk to Marie. I mean, what's the point of working for your aunt if she isn't invested in your…"

I immediately stop listening.

Zoe's invocation of nepotism *is* annoying, but I'm truly distracted away from her words because I catch a whiff of an overly flowery perfume.

I recognize it as Sydney's a moment before I take her in —maybe it's weird that I can recognize her scent after being lab partners only once, but I'm glad for it because there's something about her current demeanor that makes me uneasy.

Her strut is determined, causing little sways of her perfectly straight hair.

I suppose her pace could be inspired by pure hunger or a desire to socialize and get a break from classes, but her gaze is fixed on Lucas, who is just up ahead.

It's not unusual for them to coexist in the same space, especially because many seniors have lunch this period, but the way she's beelining toward him makes me think she's on a deliberate mission.

And it's not a comforting thought.

Lucas, of course, is unaware of her approach behind him.

I get a glimpse of his side profile as he laughs at something Daniel says, then a view of his entire light expression when he knocks him with his elbows, and the gesture throws Lucas off-balance enough that they both shift sideways in the crowd.

Sydney follows their pattern, suddenly veering to the left.

I can't see her eyes from my vantage point, but I'd be willing to bet all the money in my savings account that they're locked on Lucas. I could be totally making this up, creating subplots in my mind, but it gives me a bad, sinking feeling in my stomach.

Although many things are uncertain in this life, I've learned I can always trust my gut.

"Kate, you missed your stop," Daphne says, tilting her head toward the library.

"I'm…going to come with you two, actually."

My words are strained and a bit unexpected—for all of us—but I keep my gaze fixed ahead, ignoring whatever look the two of them share.

"Are you okay?" Daphne asks in concern.

"Yep," I answer as dismissively as I can.

I don't tell either of them what has spurred this sudden and very drastic change in habit.

They wouldn't understand.

Since it's absolutely not my place to share Lucas's business regarding his breakup with Sydney, they might mistakenly think I am jealous or being the paranoid girlfriend.

I'm neurotic enough on my own *without* adding Lucas to the mix.

However, my intention right now is innocent—I want to stay close and pay attention so I can potentially save my fake boyfriend from an embarrassing situation in front of everyone in the cafeteria.

As a bonus, since I'm so invested in my purpose for being here, I don't register the itchiness that comes with being in such a loud and crowded space. In fact, I'm not even aware of anyone else as I stick close to Zoe and Daphne and move through the lunch line.

They both select questionable-looking pasta dishes, but given I'm pairing yet another peanut butter sandwich with a leftover cheesy pastry from Books & Beans, I'm not in a place to judge the menu.

"Do you want to sit with us?" Daphne asks as we dodge a few eager freshmen looking to score the last slices of pizza.

"Of course."

"Good," Daphne says with a tentative smile.

I follow her lead to a vacant table near the far wall.

There seems to be a bit of a hierarchy to the cafeteria or, at least, some well-established claim of ownership over tables. Most of the seniors sit in the prime real estate, right next to the windows to soak up the incoming sunshine, but we're tucked away a little bit as some of the other RA members fill out our table.

"Where else would I go?" I ask as we settle in.

My spot on the bench just so happens to give me a perfect line of sight to the table where Lucas and his team-mates are arranged.

"Um, with your boyfriend?" Zoe scoffs, gesturing vaguely to where I'm already looking.

"I'm good here."

When Lucas and I were negotiating this fake-dating arrangement, I was very adamant about using this time as I normally do, hiding away in the library, but I guess his recent vulnerability—and my sudden desire to protect him —has overruled that.

I don't want to think about what that means.

"Are you two in a fight or something?" Zoe fishes. "Is this why you have suddenly come out of your cave to stare him down?"

I meet her eyes. "No."

"Are you sure?"

"I just…wanted to see something."

She quirks an eyebrow, waiting for me to elaborate.

But I ignore her and focus on very, *very* slowly removing my lunch items from my bag, taking my time arranging them on a napkin as I desperately wait for a change in subject.

Thankfully, I don't have to wait long.

"Oh, you're here?" Austin asks in amusement, tossing their *Frozen* lunchbox on the table.

"Austin," Daphne says in a warning tone.

"I mean…uh, hey, Kate."

"Hey," I return. "Nice lunchbox."

Austin gives me a pointed eyeroll. "My sister had a meltdown this morning because she wanted to take mine to school instead for who the hell knows what reason. A pre-caffeinated me cannot handle the tears of a seven-year-old, and she knows it. Obviously, I gave in."

"Oh, I get that." Daphne laughs as she twirls her fork in her pasta. "My younger sister is a terror, and I avoid her at all costs. Actually, I do that with most of my siblings."

"Don't slander your family like that," Zoe cuts in. "I happen to find fake pouting to be freaking adorable."

"Easy for you to say," Daphne retorts. "That's your signature move."

I let out a small breath, grateful that the conversation has been taken over by sibling complaints—which I can't relate to in any way—and pick at my sandwich while I resume staring at Lucas.

A vainer version of myself would feel self-conscious about my gawking, but it's not like I'm sitting here and just drooling over the way his back muscles move as he shifts in his seat or how lovely his hand is as he sweeps it through his hair...

I mean, I've held his fingers in mine and spent hours watching him at practice and at work on my car, so I'm quite familiar with them by now.

It's not our recent proximity that's catching me up, it's...something else.

Fondness, maybe?

Or some sort of obligation I feel to look out for him?

Actually, I think it's just mutual respect, which is a good trait to have in every type of relationship—even fake ones.

I scan the entirety of the cafeteria, taking in the surroundings I rarely find myself in.

Student-made signs advertise various club activities, including my crappy black and white RA poster, but I only take a passing interest in the rest, which are a minor detour on my hunt for Sydney.

It doesn't take me long to find her sitting with a group of her friends, engaging in what appears to be happy chatter while she steals glances at Lucas every ten seconds or so.

I don't know how any of this stuff is supposed to work.

In romance novels, we don't usually get to learn about the people who were involved before, so for all I know, it might be perfectly logical she's still hanging onto feelings for a high school relationship months after the fact.

It doesn't seem like it, though.

And Lucas doesn't even notice the weight of her stare, going about his lunch period as normal.

I squint to try and make out what kind of chips he's eating, and in the process, I lock eyes with Daniel.

"Guh," I breathe as his expression lights up in surprise.

They're too far away for me to catch their verbal exchange, but I infer from the way Daniel smiles at Lucas, then the way Lucas abruptly turns to look at me, that I've been discovered.

There's no hesitation in the way he scoops up his belongings and heads my direction, and Sydney looks like she's about to get up to follow him out until she realizes his destination.

And my presence.

"Hey," Lucas says as he approaches with Daniel following closely behind.

He's got a strange ability to put the weight of everything between us in that one word—like he's questioning my presence here and amused by it at the same time.

I force a smile. "Hey."

"I never thought I'd see the day when you'd step foot in the cafeteria," he teases, dropping down onto the bench beside me.

"Yeah, well…" I quickly realize I have no ready-made excuse, and I can't very well tell him that I'm here to run interference on his behalf if needed. "Today's the day."

Daphne offers him a nod of welcome, covering her mouth as she chews through a bite. "Welcome."

"You have perfect timing, Lucas," Zoe jumps in. "We were *just* talking about you."

Austin huffs out a laugh. "We were?"

"Uh-huh," my best friend says.

"What about me?" Daniel says, nudging for the person sitting beside Austin to make room for him.

Zoe awards him with a charming smile. "You're going on spring break, too, right? Up to Erie?"

"Of course," Daniel tells her proudly. "I'm counting down until we head up."

"Me, too," Daphne admits. "I could use a break from this place, even for just a few days."

Daniel gives Austin a pointed look. "Are you coming?"

"To what?" Austin asks flatly.

"To the indoor-waterpark-slash-baseball extravaganza!"

"I didn't realize it was a whole 'extravaganza,'" Daphne deadpans.

"Oh, yes," Daniel confirms proudly. "It definitely is."

"I already have plans." Austin pastes on a big, dramatic frown. "What a shame."

I smile, glad someone feels the same way I do.

"What are they?" Zoe challenges, taking a loud bite of a celery stalk as she stares them down. "Your plans?"

"My family is going to Florida."

"Lame." Daniel shakes his head. "You're totally missing out."

Austin sighs, zipping up the lunchbox. "While I don't think Florida is exactly a welcoming hub at the moment, I'd rather eat Dole Whip and follow my sister around the parks than be subjected to baseball culture."

Daniel acts completely affronted, mouth dropping open and hands in the air. "What?"

Zoe rolls her eyes, clearly ready to get back to her own agenda, and she turns her attention back to Lucas. "So."

He quirks a brow. "So?"

"I need your help convincing Kate to make the trip up north with us." She gives him puppy dog eyes and that pout she loves so much. "Please?"

I groan internally as I take another bite of my sandwich, hoping to stall for time until I have to contribute to this discussion.

"Kate has to work," Lucas tells her. "And we have plans."

"You do?" Zoe asks.

I blink as I swallow because that's news to me.

Lucas nods as he wraps his arm around my waist, pulling me close, and it's almost stupid how perfectly we fit together. "We're working on her car together."

"Oh, that's actually kind of sweet." Zoe sighs. "But surely that's not going to take *all* week?"

"Sorry, Zoe," I say with a shrug.

"You're playing, though, right?" Zoe asks Lucas.

He nods. "I am. But I'm not going up as early as the rest of the guys."

"And I'm not going at all," I pipe up.

Her nostrils flare. "But this is our last trip together!"

Daphne nudges her girlfriend with her elbow. "Really? All those plans for next year canceled?"

"Well…" Zoe's forehead pinches as she figures out how to rephrase. "The last one as seniors. Our last big hurrah before we all graduate and move on."

"Have there been any hurrahs ever?" I retort, earning a chuckle from Lucas and Austin.

"Kate," Zoe whines in exasperation, putting her palms on the table. "I know for a fact that Books & Beans is pretty much dead the week of spring break with everyone out of town. So, I'm sure Marie and the rest of the staff can handle you missing a few shifts."

I set down my pitiful lunch and wipe my hands on a napkin, giving myself time to consider.

I'm surprising myself that I'm not outright declining, but Daphne's earlier point of getting a change of scenery doesn't seem like the most awful thing.

Because aside from school field trips and the whirlwind twenty-four-hour trip to New York to scope out Columbia, I haven't been outside of my hometown.

Although the proposed trip is in the opposite direction of where I want to go in life, I suppose, in theory, it would be nice to take a detour and see what life is like elsewhere —even if that life temporarily consists of a waterpark and baseball.

Zoe is right—work is always quiet the week of spring break.

I'll definitely miss out on the bit of hourly pay, but a lack of foot traffic means no tips, and that's where the real money is.

Lucas rubs his thumb up and down my ribs, still holding me to him. "I mean, if you really want to go with me, we could drive up late Friday afternoon, then, depending on how things go—"

"Oh, we're going to win everything," Daniel cuts in. "So, we'll definitely be there until Sunday."

Lucas ignores him and addresses me. "It's a little up in the air. I know some people are getting there earlier and staying longer, but we don't have to."

It's the *we* I get snagged on.

"Regardless, it's going to be a massive party," Daniel says. "You can't miss it, Kate."

My eye twitches at the thought of that along with the expectant gazes of the people in my proximity.

I tug at the ends of my hair as I take a deep breath, trying to calm myself, but just as I shift to refocus on Lucas, I catch sight of Sydney.

And the narrow-eyed gaze she's sending my direction reminds me of the entire purpose of my being here.

"So, is everyone going?" I ask cautiously. "The usual crowd of people at practice and whatnot?"

"Yes," Zoe says enthusiastically. "Daniel's right. It will be so much fun!"

For her, I know, but for me...

"You really don't have to," Lucas says quietly.

"You should, though," Zoe presses. "It'll be good for you."

"Peer pressure." Daphne rolls her eyes. "You don't have to give in, Kate."

"I know I don't have to," I admit. "But I'll talk to Aunt Marie tonight and see what I can do."

I'm deferring the decision until later, but it seems to satisfy everyone for now.

And so I spend the rest of the lunch hour taking a passing interest in conversation, imagining all sorts of scenarios of this trip, and leaning into Lucas's hold.

TWELVE

"Looks nice," Lucas says as we walk up to the hotel.

At first glance, the building itself looks to be about six stories high, and the tubes of some of the twisty slides from the indoor park wrap around the outside of the building. It seems to be a smart use of space, but I wonder if riders feel a blast of cold in the winters through the thick plastic.

That aside, I just can't believe I'm here.

After a week of Books & Beans and minimal interaction with Lucas, I'm now going from zero to sixty. Despite him telling Zoe that we had plans to work on his car, he did all of it on his own but sent me progress pictures.

Yesterday, he showed up near the end of my shift and got to chatting with my aunt about his plans for the weekend.

Aunt Marie was only too happy to encourage me into doing some "normal teenage activities," according to her, so she's covering for me, which isn't too much of a strain for one weekend because, as predicted, it's been pretty dead all week.

There's something about Lucas that makes me want to step outside my comfort zone, and before our fake relationship, I would have never done anything like this.

It's terrifying, exhilarating, and mind-boggling all at once.

"You're sure you're okay with this?" Lucas asks.

I let out a small laugh. "Ignoring the fact that this is the eighth time you've asked me, it'd be pretty crappy of me to tell you I want to back out *now*, given that we just drove for two hours."

"I guess you're right." Lucas's smile widens as he reaches for my bag. "Here, let me get that."

"I've got it," I say, turning away slightly and gripping the strap. "You've got enough stuff of your own to worry about."

He has his very sleek suitcase—likely containing his swimsuit, casual clothes, and toiletries—and his equipment bag, which is so heavy that I could barely move it when I tried to shove it over to fit my stuff in the backseat.

"Okay," Lucas relents as we head inside.

The scent of chlorine is overwhelming, growing more pronounced as we cross the tile floor and head toward the elevators, even though we can't even see any water features from the lobby.

I glance at the vacant check-in desk. "Don't we need to—"

"Hey, man!" Daniel calls as he approaches.

"Hey," Lucas replies, eyeing his friend. "How's it going?"

Daniel is wearing what must be the smallest swim shorts known to humankind.

Lucas is better at withholding his reaction, but I feel myself blush as I pointedly look anywhere but at him, settling on the clean, dark tile floor and my scuffed-up shoes.

"It's going so, so good, dude. Greene lost today, so we're already in a good position for our doubleheader tomorrow."

"*If* we win the morning game," Lucas amends.

"Don't put that energy out in the world. Ugh." Daniel shakes his entire body in disgust, which I, unfortunately, can see in my peripheral vision. "We're the best in our district."

"Not in the state, though," Lucas argues. "We're not getting on base enough right now."

Daniel rolls his eyes. "Numbers only go so far."

I mentally will this conversation to speed up as I shift on my feet.

Lucas must pick up on my restlessness—or maybe he's just ready to move on himself—because he smoothly extracts us from our present company.

"Well, I think we'll get settled," he tells his teammate. "You've got our room key?"

"Our?" I gulp, shooting a panicked look at Lucas.

I assumed I'd be staying with Zoe and Daphne, given that they invited me, but as I think about it...

I'm an idiot.

Because why would any couple in high school turn down the opportunity to be alone and unsupervised?

"It'll be fine," Lucas says quickly and quietly.

"Oh, yeah." Daniel digs in his pocket—which is far too close to the bulge at the front of his trunks for my liking—and pulls out a key card. "Here you go."

Lucas accepts it with a nod. "Thanks."

"Everyone's already down in the water," Daniel adds as we step away. "Come find us after you have your *alone* time. The park's open twenty-four seven, so there's no real rush."

I frown at his implication, but Lucas seems unbothered by it as he calls for the elevator.

I know he doesn't expect *that* from me in any way, shape, or form, but I never considered that other people might think that's what we're doing.

I'm no innocent—well, my brain isn't, with help from books I've read—but I haven't put much thought into people my age having casual sex.

At least, not when I can help it.

Zoe has always been an oversharer, and I've never wanted to scrub my brain clean more than when she went into way too much detail about the first time she and Daphne hooked up.

But now, as Lucas slides the key into the slot to open the door, all I can think about is his experience.

And my lack thereof.

"Not bad," he says, appraising the space.

I don't care about the color of the carpet or the artwork on the walls because I'm still fixated on my thoughts and imagining what it would feel like to have his hands on my bare skin...

Distracted, I walk forward until my shins hit the edge of the bed.

The *one* bed.

"Oh, no," I groan.

Lucas drops his bag on the ground. "What?"

I can't hide my abject horror at the oversized piece of furniture that's impossible to miss.

"The one bed trope," I rasp, knowing my eyes are wide.

"Is there a trope for every situation?" Lucas asks playfully, oblivious to my inner panic.

I'm grateful for that because the thought of him knowing what was just rolling through my mind is enough to make my cheeks burn.

"It's a very popular mechanism," I tell him, trying to remain calm and casual. "Two people who don't like each other show up somewhere, and there is only one place for them to sleep. Usually, they argue and end up with some sort of pillow barrier that gives way in the middle of the night. Or something happens, and they end up together."

Lucas removes his hat and runs a hand through his hair, considering my words. "There's a problem with your theory."

"No. There isn't. It's a perfectly common scenario in the romance genre. Trust me."

"It doesn't apply here," he protests, smiling wide and showing off that one dimple. "Because I like you."

I'm suddenly at a loss for words.

"And there's more than enough space for two people in here," Lucas says before he makes a big show of flinging himself on the bed.

The sight of him sprawled out on the huge bed is a little childish, but I also find it just a little bit adorable.

Most importantly, though, how calm he seems about this entire situation puts me a little more at ease.

"See?" Lucas says, moving his limbs like he's making a snow angel. "Plenty of room."

I tug the ends of my hair as I glance around, wishing there was a couch or furniture other than a desk that could be used as an adequate sleeping spot.

He jumps up and bats away my fingers before sliding his own at the base of my neck.

"What are you doing?" I ask, jerking away.

"Whenever you're stressing about something, you pull at your hair," Lucas says as he starts to press gentle circles against my skin.

I do.

I know I do.

But I didn't know Lucas did.

"I think it's a subconscious movement to release tension," he continues. "But I think this might actually help you instead."

And he's right.

I swallow as I relax a little bit more, focusing on the heat and the spearmint and the proximity.

The sensation I usually feel when I'm anxious—the slight burning in my chest and tightness in my arms—surfaces, but it transforms into something warm and delicious and addicting.

The blood rushes to my face as I register just exactly *what* this is.

Flutters of attraction.

Actually, that's not doing what I'm feeling justice.

It's more like getting warmed by a fire until there's no other option but to give in and melt.

I turn my head sideways enough to look at the lines of concentration in his features, and it's a little devastating that he's so collected at this moment.

I clear my throat and step away, trying to spare my ego and distance myself from him. "Okay. I think the tension has been released."

Lucas drops his hand. "If you're sure."

"Yep," I say, voice a little higher than normal. "Should we get ready and join everyone else?"

After all, that's why we're here.

He chuckles and reaches for his bag. "You're becoming more social by the day, Kate. Never thought I'd see it happen."

I frown as I wrestle my bikini out from my bag. "I'll go, uh, get changed."

"Okay."

I let out a breath of relief as I close the bathroom door behind me, shutting him out and whatever *that* was.

I toss my bathing suit pieces on the counter so I can press my palms against the cool surface, needing a beat to collect myself. The fact that my thoughts were on intimate acts right as we walked into a one bed trope situation...

I'm becoming a horrible cliché.

Not that there's anything wrong with a well-timed familiar sequence of events, but—I remind myself as I stare at my reflection—this isn't a book.

This is real life.

And right now, there's a gorgeous guy stripping down on the other side of the door.

Oh, god, what if he's wearing a similar suit to Daniel's?

I think I would combust on the spot.

I splash cold water on my face, trying to bring myself under control, but my effort has no measurable impact.

My hands shake as I peel off my clothes and replace them with the bikini I've had since Zoe's pool party freshman year, and it's surprisingly held up nicely in the bottom drawer of my dresser.

It's plain, black, and simple, and I actually think it looks okay.

I twist to the side, catching my reflection and ensuring I'm still covered on the bottom before I adjust the top as much as I can. My boobs have gone up a cup size since I started high school, and while I'm not in danger of spilling out, everything on top is a bit snug and attention-drawing.

And I stupidly left the cover-up—a large, old t-shirt—in my bag.

"You good?" I call, hand hovering over the knob.

"Yeah," Lucas returns.

I open the door and step out, intending to recover my modesty as quickly as possible, but I stop short.

I get a flash of Lucas's back before he tugs his shirt back on, and I gulp at the brief sight of his muscles.

I'm glad I'm taking him in now, alone and unjudged, and I give myself permission to appraise him slowly until he turns.

But what I didn't anticipate was his reaction to *me*.

I've never really understood the phrase "his eyes darken," a mainstay in steamy romance, but now, I absolutely do.

Although, perhaps a more apt description is that his

lids narrow and his gaze intensifies as he takes in a sharp breath.

Whatever it is, it's flattering.

And it makes my heart pound wildly in my chest.

"Um, I'm just going to…" I stumble forward toward my belongings and find the prized item of clothing, which I pull on as fast as I can. "You ready?"

He nods and follows me wordlessly as we head out the way we came.

Once we've made it back to the lobby, we follow the signs down two hallways until we reach the main doors to the waterpark, and we present our room key in order to get bracelets from the bored employee manning the entrance, and then we're in.

The exterior I took in from the parking lot doesn't do this place justice—it's even more massive than I thought.

It's not just a big body of water, though. There are at least four different pools, one lazy river, an area that looks like a water-based jungle gym, a multitude of slides, a water volleyball court, and a ton of seating and lounge chairs for when people are ready for a break.

"What do you want to do first?" Lucas asks.

"Oh, uh…" I kick my sandals off. "Whatever."

"Kate!" Zoe screams. "Get over here! Lazy river time!"

She, Daphne, and a few of our classmates are snagging clear inner tubes from the massive pile at the edge of the pool.

"I guess I'm going that way," I tell Lucas. "You can find your friends if you want. Don't feel obligated to hang around with me."

He tilts his head. "I love a good obligation."

I let out a nervous laugh as we join the group.

And the water washes away everything I'm overthinking.

It remains that way for the rest of the afternoon.

After a few spins around the lazy river, Lucas's teammates find us and insist that we have to try out all the slides. It's kind of funny because most of them were clearly made with kids in mind, but Daniel and the other guys scream in excitement as they twist and turn through the passages.

Next, I begrudgingly join in on a water volleyball match but spend most of the time treading water and floating while Lucas spares me from any actual gameplay.

Finally, after the sun sets and the blue pool lights kick on, we break for a dinner that consists of cheese pizza, french fries, and other easy-make fried food from the concession stand.

I'm so exhausted from all the social interaction and physical exertion of the day that I give up on the brownie Lucas and I have been splitting and slip out.

I leave behind the increasingly rowdy group and grab a stack of towels to wrap up in. I pick a lounge chair that's a few rows away from passing traffic, then I cocoon myself in the cotton and do some breathing exercises.

The sounds of splashing and people in the near distance are tolerable, and it's enough of a white noise that I'm not missing my headphones at the moment.

"Comfortable?" Lucas drawls as he joins me.

I glance up at him. "Very."

He pulls another seat closer, then adjusts the back of it so we'll be level, and he falls onto it.

I burrow deeper, watching as he arranges his lone towel to act as a blanket for himself, and let out a yawn.

"I'm sure I'll see plenty of that tomorrow," he says in a teasing tone. "After hours and hours of baseball. If we win, we'll play again in the afternoon, then on Sunday morning."

I smile. "A steep price to pay, but I'm committed to playing the doting girlfriend."

Lucas huffs a laugh before he pops the rest of the brownie in his mouth.

We're both nearly horizontal, lying side by side on our respective chairs, but I'm curled up to face him while he watches two parents try to wrangle their toddler and remove their floaties.

The air is slightly muggy from the heat of the water, and I still haven't gotten used to the chlorine, but it's peaceful to be here.

To listen to the background noise of families.

To sit still and relax in a new place.

To be by Lucas's side.

I fight the heaviness of my eyelids as hard as I can, watching the rise and fall of his chest, but eventually, I drift off to sleep.

THIRTEEN

"You sure you're not too tired to drive?" I ask Lucas as he takes a sip of coffee.

It's not as good as what we make at Books & Beans or even what his mom has at home, but this gas station brew is giving us both a bit of a boost as we pack up for the ride back.

"I'm good," Lucas says.

His tone isn't exactly clipped, but it's not the friendly one I'm familiar with either.

It is, however, understandable.

After waking up late and in somewhat of a panic on our lounge chairs, he rushed to meet his teammates and prepare, setting a not-so-great tone for the day ahead.

Even with a bit of a rocky start and the opposing team scoring two runs early on, Lucas and his teammates pulled through in the ninth inning, leaving most of the spectators on the edge of their seats.

Unfortunately, after that victory, in the next game they got slaughtered and knocked out of the tournament.

While I can't totally empathize, not being an athletic or competitive person myself, I don't like seeing him sad or introspective or whatever emotion this is.

He was the one who suggested we head home tonight, even though his teammates plan to heal their wounds by partying and swimming for another day.

I'm certainly not going to complain.

The break of routine was nice for a little while, but I think if I had my choice of destination, I would have picked, like, a remote island or cabin in the woods away from the chaos.

Now, though, as the passenger, I have nothing to fixate on but the road signs we pass as we head home, and it's a nice reprieve.

I do wish we were driving slow enough for me to crack the window and let my hand ride the current of the air, but Lucas is pushing us along at a solid seventy-two miles per hour, so I keep my window up and my arms crossed over my chest.

We ride in relative and comfortable silence, music playing low, and the minutes fly by until the sun disappears into the horizon.

It's strange how the ride up to Erie felt like it took so long because as we pull up to my house, it seems like it's been all of ten minutes—instead of two hours—since I slid into the passenger seat.

I unbuckle and glance over at Lucas, debating on whether to offer some comforting words or say *something* before I get out of the car.

But instead of the contemplative and slightly pinched expression I've been taking in since we got in the car, his gaze is wrinkled with confusion and fixed over my shoulder and out the window.

Lucas squints. "Is that...?"

He quickly cuts the engine and is out of his seatbelt and the car before I can even turn to see what he's looking at.

And when I finally do, I'm utterly horrified.

Because it's not the somewhat harmless sight of a door ajar.

It's the shadow of a person—my mother, to be precise—sprawled out on the small square of cement by our front door, barely illuminated by a flickering lightbulb.

"Mom," I shout in a mixture of panic and annoyance.

"Kate," she says groggily.

"What's going on?" I ask, kneeling by her side. "Are you okay?"

She bats her palm against my face like she's trying to placate me, and it's very off-putting in combination with her sudden bought of maniacal laughter.

I flinch away from the contact, and her arm falls back onto the ground.

"I think she was trying to get in," Lucas murmurs.

He leans forward to turn the key in the lock—who knows how long it's just been sitting in the door.

I squeeze my eyes closed for just a second, trying to stave off the total mortification I feel, then refocus on the task at hand.

"Mom, let's get you inside," I say evenly.

I stagger and stumble as I try to figure out the best way

to get her up, given that she's basically splayed out and dead weight.

My movements are *not* graceful.

I try to heave her up by her hands, putting all my weight into leveraging her up, but she fights my efforts.

She flails like an irritated toddler, so I release her and simply scowl down at her with my hands on my hips.

"Do you want me to help?" Lucas asks quietly.

I cannot muster the courage to look at him and see whatever expression of pity or shock is on his features, and when I open my mouth to decline his offer, no words make it out.

My mother reacts to his presence, though, blinking rapidly up at him. "Who're you?"

"Lucas," he answers in a gentle tone. "Kate's boyfriend."

I press my lips together, giving no verbal confirmation as I watch her glassy eyes move between us.

She manages more laughter, but this time it's a snort-chuckle that turns into a round of coughing.

I let it roll for a few beats until I grow concerned she's about to throw up all over my shoes.

Lucas doesn't seem to share the same worry as he bends down, meeting her at eye level. "Can I help you?"

When she doesn't give any sort of verbal deterrent, he scoops her up into his arms.

He nods toward the door. "Do you mind?"

I shake myself out of my stupor to open it, giving him room to gingerly step inside with my mother in his arms.

Lucky for me, it seems like the peak of my embarrassment has passed.

She's contentedly passed out against his chest instead of babbling about who knows what like she usually does in this state.

I lead Lucas to her bedroom, which is in complete disarray.

The condition is almost laughable, given the lack of furniture in here—the mattress is directly on the floor, and all of her clothes are in a pile at the bottom of the closet—but I frown as I spot some of the books that went missing from my room strewn on the floor.

Lucas gets her settled onto her bed, then backs out of the room to give us privacy.

I debate whether to change her clothes and make her more comfortable in a sleep shirt, but I ultimately decide that it's not worth the hassle.

It's not like she'll feel it.

Or appreciate it when she wakes up again.

Instead, I wrench off her strappy-heeled sandals, which are tight enough to leave marks in her skin, then arrange her unconscious form so she's on her side before covering her with a blanket.

I sigh as I pull back.

Part of me knows that after years of this type of behavior, I shouldn't feel bad for her, but I can't help it.

I don't know if it's some sort of generic obligation or just a practical one, knowing that she needs help, but I do.

It doesn't mean anything about this is easy or how I would choose to go about things if I had my way.

I shut her door as I exit, then move down the hall, intending to get my bag from the car and dismiss Lucas as quickly as possible, but I don't make it past my bedroom.

Because he's sitting on the edge of my bed, gripping his thighs as he stares at the floor and my bag, which he, apparently, had the forethought to retrieve while I was dealing with my mother.

I can't even imagine what he's thinking at this moment.

And honestly, I'm not sure I want to.

"Thanks for your help," I say as confidently as I can. "You can—"

"How often does that happen?" Lucas asks sharply.

I bite the edge of my lip before I answer. "Often enough."

Lucas lets out a breath as he stands, then he frowns down at me. "You shouldn't have to deal with that."

"I know. But that doesn't change anything."

"Why don't you live with your aunt?"

I run my fingers through my hair and yank on the ends, trying to vent my frustration in a way that doesn't involve a complete emotional breakdown.

Remembering his gentle care and recognition of this behavior, I drop my hands.

"It's complicated," I whisper as my throat tightens.

Lucas doesn't fire back right away or ask another question that I definitely don't want to answer.

But the way he's looking at me—eyes wide, corners of his mouth turned down, head shaking—is worse than any conversation.

"I'm okay," I assure him. "You can get out of here."

"Is that what you want?" He crosses his arms over his chest. "You want to be alone?"

"Yes."

I don't believe it myself.

And I don't think he does either.

His eyes search mine as he lets out a long exhale. "You can let me in, you know."

It's a good line, but there's something about it that makes me laugh—maybe it's my reaction to this whole thing or the helplessness I feel, but I can't help the bitter sound.

"Oh, you're in," I say, throwing my hands up in a gesture to the shambles of my surroundings. "You're *so* in, Lucas."

He frowns and shakes his head. "I'm not, Kate. We've spent so much time together over these past few weeks, but you've never opened up. I mean, I had no idea that you were…dealing with stuff at home."

"Well, congratulations," I say flatly. "You've gotten the privilege of seeing my real life. Even though I didn't want you to."

As soon as the words spill out, I want to take them back.

Even with my inner turmoil rolling, I know I'm being too harsh to someone who just wants to help.

Because I'd do the same for him.

"I'm sorry," I say genuinely, wringing my hands. "I'm just mad and embarrassed and deflecting."

"I get it." Lucas unfolds his arms and sticks his hands in his pockets. "I mean, I didn't exactly want to share everything with my messed up family."

"The consequences of a fake relationship, I guess."

Something flashes over his features, and I absolutely don't have the capacity to try and decipher what it means.

"Well, I'll leave you to it, then," Lucas says after a beat. "Thanks for coming with me. I am…really glad you did."

"I am, too."

Because despite getting a little overwhelmed and his loss and all of *this*, I actually really enjoyed the trip with him.

And that's why, I think, when he brushes by me, I grab his wrist without a shred of hesitation.

"Will you stay?"

As I ask the question, I realize the only thing that would be more devastating than everything that has happened in front of him since we got here would be to face the rest of tonight alone.

Vulnerability is a bitch.

But so is loneliness.

Lucas seems almost relieved at my request—his expression softens, and the tension leaves his body as he nods.

"I'll grab my stuff from the car."

I nod, then scramble to get through my nighttime routine of teeth-brushing, face-washing, and pulling on the old ratty sweatpants and t-shirt I never got the chance to wear last night.

He comes back moments later and slips into the bathroom, performing his own ablutions as I ready my bed and slide in.

I fluff the two small pillows before covering myself with the sheet and blanket, thanking my past self for washing them just before I left.

I hold my breath as Lucas returns to my room and try not to have a mental freakout at the realization that I am about to sleep with a boy for the first time.

My worries and inner thoughts are quieted as he closes the door behind him, ignoring the fact that I did a ridiculous duct tape patch job on the bottom of it.

This is Lucas.

He's kind, thoughtful, considerate.

And I feel safe with him.

"You okay?" Lucas asks as he gets settled beside me.

It's much smaller than the hotel bed we could have shared. We're both on our sides, facing each other, and we're close enough that I can smell the fresh mint of his toothpaste.

"I think so," I answer. "But I'm sure this wasn't what you planned for a spring break trip."

Lucas reaches over to tuck my hair behind my ear. "I don't know about that."

"What do you mean?"

"I was promised a one bed trope," he says softly. "And you've delivered."

I hum as I fight off a smile.

And we eventually both slip into a peaceful and undisturbed sleep.

FOURTEEN

Lucas dangles my own car keys in front of me.

It's a simple silver key and fob fixed onto a little coffee mug keychain from Books & Beans, but the meaning behind the gesture is just now hitting me.

I should have expected this, given that I've held up my end of our deal and he's been diligently working on this since the beginning, but he's done just shy of our two-month deadline.

"It's really ready?" I ask dumbly.

The question is stupid because Lucas brought me to his house for this specific reason, and I can see my little Toyota with my own eyes. I'm close enough, standing beside it in his garage, that I could press my hand against the hood.

It does, however, look drastically different from the last time I saw it.

For one, it's actually put back together, but aside from that, there's less rust and fewer dents than there used to

161

be. He couldn't manage the miracle of getting all of them out, but I'm impressed.

I don't know anything about cars, obviously, but it's crazy that something can go from being in pieces to totally put back together.

That sentiment might also be true for people.

At least, it is for me.

Since Lucas stayed over, something has shifted between us.

Not drastically, like tearing apart an engine or transmission or whatever the hell he did, but there's a difference in our interactions, like they're somehow more tentative and impactful at the same time.

It's been…more than nice.

We've continued the charade of our fake relationship with ease, but, per our original agreement, it would seem it has run its course.

I suppose the end was inevitable, but it feels real now that I'm holding my keys again.

"It's ready," Lucas confirms proudly.

I press my nervous fingers into the body, then move around to inspect the passenger door and step closer to him, wondering if this is really it between us.

Something just feels unfinished—and it's not my car.

"You did more than we bargained for," I murmur.

He shrugs, watching me take in his work. "It was easy."

"I don't believe that. But I appreciate it nonetheless. It's going to be strange to start driving on my own again." I bite the edge of my mouth. "Kind of like riding a bike, right? Will pick it up again eventually."

"You know, I was thinking…what if things don't change?"

My heart jumps in my chest, but I try to maintain outward composure. "What do you mean?"

Lucas slides his hands into his pockets.

I think he's trying to come off as unbothered, just like I am, but I recognize the signs of tenseness. He's holding his posture slightly rigid, shoulders hunched and jaw tight as he meets my eyes.

"What if we kept doing this?" He pauses for emphasis. "Dating, I mean."

I swallow and choose my next words carefully. "Is that what you want?"

"Yes," Lucas says without any hesitation. "I've thought about it, and I can't find one reason we shouldn't."

I can feel my pulse in my ears. "This was supposed to be temporary."

"I know."

"This isn't how fake dating is supposed to work."

Lucas chuckles and runs a hand through his hair. "I don't think it's been *fake* for me for a while now."

I lean against the car, needing something to steady my body as my mind races. "You're telling me that you want to date me for real? Like, not just me sitting at your practices and games? Not being seen together in public just to draw attention?"

"No offense, but you haven't been doing the best job of that anyway."

"Hey," I protest, managing a slight smile.

He laughs more freely. "Do you have any other objections?"

I consider it. "Well, in the books, we're supposed to have a big, dramatic falling-out in front of everyone, so they all find out we've been faking it, and everything blows up in our faces."

"That sounds terrible."

"But it's usually how it goes."

"There's nothing that needs to be 'usual' about this," Lucas argues. "I mean, this isn't a book, Kate. This is *us*."

"I know," I huff. "It's just hard to operate without a roadmap."

He snorts. "Do we really need one?"

I shift on my feet, considering the question. "I mean, how do we know how to handle things? And do we need some sort of plan? Like, do we only continue dating until school ends? Or go through the summer? We'll both be off to college in the fall."

"What if we just take it day by day?" Lucas suggests.

"Day by day," I repeat.

"Nothing much has to change."

My eyes widen. "Nothing *much* has to change?"

He pushes off to step in front of me, taking both my hands in his as he meets my eyes.

And it's at this moment that I accept a truth I haven't given myself permission to.

I *like* Lucas Hunt.

A lot.

There's no reason not to.

Especially when he smiles at me with that damn dimple.

It should be a comforting and very welcome sight, reassuring me we're making the right decision, but that night at my house was only a glimpse of what my life is like and why I am the way that I am, and I want to be honest with him.

If we're going to do this, I think he should know what he's in for with me.

"Lucas, I just feel like I should warn you about something," I tell him as confidently as I can. "Before we do this. I mean, really do this, you know?"

He rubs his thumbs over my knuckles. "What is it, Kate?"

"I have issues," I blurt.

"Don't we all?" Lucas murmurs.

I focus on my breath and the way our hands feel clasped together before I find the confidence to speak again.

"I have a lot of anxiety," I explain quietly. "It's mostly tied up in stuff with my mom, which I guess isn't that surprising. For a while I had a therapist, but she stopped taking on pro bono work, so I've been trying coping mechanisms on my own. But it kind of manifests into sensory issues, which is why I have the headphones and am practically allergic to sound, and...I just have issues."

Lucas hasn't wavered for one single second throughout my rambling. "So?"

"None of that stuff bothers you? I mean, this certainly isn't what you had planned to deal with while finishing out your senior year."

"I definitely didn't plan on you," he says, taking a step forward.

Lucas drops his grasp on both my hands to cup my chin.

I've read enough to pick up on the signal of what is

about to happen, but I don't anticipate the reaction that bubbles up inside me.

The millisecond his lips meet mine, fireworks erupt in my body, wreaking havoc on my bloodstream, my limbs, my rationale.

All I can do is reach forward and put my hands on his chest to hold myself steady as I give in to the rhythm he's setting.

I'm along for the ride, trying to mimic his movements.

His lips are firm and warm and gentle and everything I would have expected.

And more.

Because nothing could have prepared me for this feeling.

That peck he gave me a few weeks ago was merely a precursor, but it's almost laughable to consider how different this is.

He kissed me then.

But he's doing something else entirely now.

"Claiming" seems like too extreme of a term, but I can't conjure any other descriptor of what's happening as we both give in to what's been building between us.

Although, maybe it's a fresh start, a declaration of intentions.

When he breaks our connection, I feel the loss immediately, but I'm grateful for a moment to catch my breath—because I have no idea how to time my inhales while trying to move my lips against his and not do something stupid like knock our noses or teeth together.

"So," Lucas says, smiling widely. "How about we make a new plan?"

I bite back my own elation, readying to lecture him on how we're supposed to have a dramatic, coming-together moment, but I decide to withhold my comment.

Because, to this point, this isn't a trope or a story.

This is just for us.

"I don't know how to do any of this," I admit. "We're resolving our core conflict before one was even created. I mean, what do we do now? Just—"

"Be happy?" Lucas suggests.

"I guess."

"Well, don't sound too excited."

"As long as we don't fall into some awful miscommunication cliché," I warn. "I hate when novels create drama just for the sake of it, you know?"

"No drama. How about we just go for a drive?"

I smile widely as I pull my keys from my pocket. "My turn to be your chauffeur, then?"

"I think I'll just call you my 'girlfriend' if you're okay with that."

I nod and give him my most genuine grin.

Because I don't think I've ever been more okay in my life than this moment.

FIFTEEN

"You've been happy today," Aunt Marie says. "Well, not just today. Lately. For weeks."

The comment comes as she slides what might be the last latte of our late morning rush across the counter, nodding to a grateful and uncaffeinated customer.

I finish wiping down the steamer, then turn to her. "I know."

For the first time in my existence, I feel that sort of giggly urge to gush.

But I don't for a number of reasons—the most pressing being that Lucas and I have been pretty public thus far, and it's kind of nice to have these memories and moments that are just between us.

"I like this version of you," she comments, tossing a pair of tongs in the sink.

I'm pretty sure she's referring to the way I haven't been able to stop smiling since I arrived this morning, zoning out in thoughts and memories of Lucas's lips on mine last night.

"Me, too," I admit.

Because I'm just a silly, sappy sucker who is falling for a guy she started fake dating.

And, honestly, I kind of love it.

Before Lucas, I hadn't given much thought to what it would be like to be with someone.

I was content to live through the fictional relationships I read about in books, but I'm very appreciative of the first-hand experience I'm getting now.

I suppose that's a very dry and unsexy way to put it, but it's true.

"You okay if I head to the back for a little bit?" Aunt Marie asks. "Jessica has some paperwork I need to put in for the new employee."

"Sure," I say, taking her place in front of the register. "Looks like we're in for a lull."

She pats me on the shoulder before she retreats, and when she's gone, I take stock of the space.

There's a young mother nursing her baby in the corner, a few college-age friends at a table in the center of the space, gushing over some new vampire romance, and an older couple sitting by the window.

I like hearing the murmurs of their conversations and the rustling of their movements, and I take a breath, knowing Aunt Marie's right.

I feel at peace, and I like it a lot.

The front bell chimes, calling for my attention, and I glance up to see a forty-something woman step in, greeting me with a wide smile as she approaches.

"Hello. Welcome." I plaster a smile on my face. "What can I get for you? Books or beans or both?"

She laughs, revealing bright white teeth that contrast with her dark red lipstick. "How many times a day do you have to say that?"

"Too many," I admit with a genuine chuckle. "Still am happy to do so, though."

"Good," she says as she adjusts her purse on her shoulder. "Because I was hoping you would be able to recommend a book or two to me."

"Of course," I tell her as I step around the counter. "What do you have in mind? A favorite author or genre I can work with?"

She shakes her head. "It's not for me. I'm looking for a gift for my daughter."

"That's very sweet of you," I say. "How old is she? Does she have any current reads or things she's into?"

"She's about your age, I'd guess," the woman says, eyes scanning me. "And, to be honest, she's not really a reader. But I think it could be a good distraction for her."

"Okay." I lead her over to one of the shelves in the corner. "Is she high school or college age?"

"High school. And, um, I can't decide if romance is a good choice for her or not. You see, she's been really down lately. She got dumped by her boyfriend, and she's pretty devastated."

"Oh, no," I groan. "I'm so sorry to hear that."

She nods as she frowns. "It's been rough, so after letting her watch every available romcom on the internet, I figure it might be time to try something else."

"I think I can help you out. And her. There's nothing like a good book boyfriend as a distraction from real life."

"Great," she says, brightening up at my words. "I like that."

I end up giving her three options—a typical high school romance with lots of swoony moments, a new adult college freshman love story, and a teenage fantasy book.

Surely, one of them will do the trick.

After that, the woman asks me to recommend some food and drinks, and after I take note of her preferences, she gives me full rein to pick my favorites.

"Here you are," I say brightly as she settles at a table. "Two chai tea lattes and some of my favorite pastries, a chocolate chip scone and our marbled chocolate brownie."

I took extra time to arrange the desserts on the plate because if her daughter is anything like most people my age who come in here, she's going to want to photograph it.

"Thank you," she says graciously.

I have to attend to more customers over the next few minutes, but I keep an eye on her while I work, eager to see the reaction of her daughter whenever she shows up.

As I wait on a couple who is very much in the handsy phase of their relationship, I see when she arrives. Out of the corner of my eye, I see them embrace, and I can't help the pangs of jealousy that hit.

I think in a different world, one where my dad didn't have a fatal heart attack in the middle of his workday, my mother and I could have been like that—or at least have had some sort of relationship that isn't totally unbalanced and harmful.

I just have a few more weeks until I turn eighteen, legally and officially responsible for my own well-being, and while I don't expect anything drastic to happen once I hit that milestone, I think mentally it'll be good for me to be out from under her control.

"Thank you," I call to the couple once the mobile payment is processed.

They both nod in gratitude before heading out, and finally, I'm able to fully take in the sight of the woman and her daughter.

I'm prepared to let the pangs of longing hit when I do, but I don't expect the feeling of my stomach dropping outside of my body.

Because it's Sydney.

Sydney Smith, right there, ten feet away.

Our eyes lock the moment she swallows a bite of brownie, and she quickly follows it up with a sip of the drink I prepared with extra love and care, thinking she really needed it.

I guess I wasn't wrong.

But it sure feels that way.

I don't know if it's karma or the universe recognizing how easy I've had it lately, but I'm slightly devastated to realize that the very nice woman I helped and chatted with is the one Lucas wants to avoid for the rest of time.

I cannot believe that I was just happily chattering with the other woman in Lucas's parents' marriage, and I feel kind of guilty thinking about how sweet and wonderful Lauren was when we met.

In fact, if I didn't know better, I'd say that Sydney's

mom actually reminds me of Lauren, which is kind of messed up.

I mutter a low string of expletives.

And then promptly find any excuse to stay busy.

I wipe the counters, rearrange the same bookmark stand I dusted last shift, and take inventory of the food in the case, even though we manage it all digitally through the checkout system.

After I finally run out of things to do, I pick up my phone.

Social media is the same as it was when I checked a few hours ago, but I groan at the sight of a message from Lucas, recalling the promise he made earlier to swing by after his game.

I frantically move to his message, then exhale in relief.

Game ran late. Okay if I come by later instead?

Before now, I was counting down the minutes until he'd make his appearance, but I'm happy that he's deviating from the original time frame.

I start and stop typing a few times, trying to decide how to word my current situation, then ultimately decide just to tell him when he arrives.

Totally fine, I respond.

Sorry! I do want to see you.

Me? Or are you hoping I'll save you some baked goods?

I was banking on my girlfriend doing that out of the goodness of her heart.

Fine, I reply, following it up with a kissy face emoji.

Apparently, I am now a person who sends those to her boyfriend.

Jane Austen would be appalled—or maybe she'd find some text-based equivalent for the Mr. Darcy hand-graze.

We won by the way.

I cringe at that message, knowing that he didn't mean anything by it, but I really should take a more active interest in things like batting averages and win streaks.

Then again, Lucas seems to like me just the way I am, so I just settle for sending a few smiley faces in celebration.

"Kate."

I nearly drop my phone at Sydney's abrupt appearance on the other side of the counter.

"Uh, hey," I say lamely, shoving it in the back pocket of my jeans. "Do you two need refills?"

She shakes her head, glancing over her shoulder at her mom before turning back to me.

"My mom told me that you picked those books and our treats, and I'm sure you didn't know it was for me, but thank you," Sydney says politely.

"You're welcome," I manage.

"They're perfect."

The smile I give her is tight.

It was much easier to be around her before Lucas and I became a real relationship, seeing her as some sort of barrier or purpose for spending time with him, but now that she's standing right in front of me with all her incorrect assumptions about him and me, I truly don't know how to feel.

Sydney flips that sheet of blonde hair of hers over her shoulder. "Look, I've been meaning to talk to you since…"

"Chemistry?" I prompt.

"I was going to say, 'Since I accosted you with my feelings for your boyfriend,'" Sydney admits, managing a hollow laugh.

I shift on my feet, unsure how to respond.

"Well, I guess I just wanted to apologize. That…what happened between us shouldn't have anything to do with you. And I'm sorry if I, like, soured anything for you." She squeezes her eyes shut briefly. "Not that I have the power to do that or whatever."

I withhold a smirk.

Because I am very familiar with putting my foot in my mouth, and it might be a little mean, but I'm actually grateful to see her anything less than perfect.

"I appreciate that," I tell her. "But, no. It's fine."

She smiles somewhat sadly. "You two look happy together. I mean, like, *really* happy."

"We are."

"It was kind of weird to see you guys at first, but I guess it was exactly the closure I needed. To see that it's real, I mean."

I nod. "It is real."

I say that just as much for her as I do for me.

"So, I guess I just wanted to say that I'm officially trying to move on. Not that you need to tell Lucas. I mean, you can tell him if you want. I've tried so many times to reach him, and the best thing I can do is to stop doing all that and let him be." She pauses and lets out a breathy laugh. "I'm rambling again."

I fidget slightly at the awkwardness, and my gaze moves over her shoulder.

Her mom smiles, waves, and mouths her gratitude,

completely oblivious to who I am and the context of the conversation happening between Sydney and me.

I do my best to give her a subtle nod.

"Well, I should get back to my mom," Sydney says, pushing off the counter. "Just...take care of him, okay? Be good to him. He deserves it."

"I will."

And it's a promise that I'll do my best to uphold.

SIXTEEN

"Oh my god, look at you!" Zoe screeches as I approach her in the stands.

And unfortunately for me, it has the effect of catching the attention of everyone in a ten-foot radius, meaning I can feel my face grow red from the attention.

I adjust the brim of Lucas's hat, the one he gave me weeks ago, as I sit down beside her.

"You're all decked out to support your man," she says, beaming.

I pull at the hem of my t-shirt, which also belongs to Lucas, and unlike the hat I can adjust, this is stuck being a few sizes too big. It's not exactly the most flattering, but it'll do.

Actually, the genuine dimpled grin he gave me from the dugout tells me all I need to know about his thoughts on my sudden foray into school spirit.

"I guess," I say, tilting my head toward her. "Oh, hey, Daphne."

She gives Zoe an annoyed look before meeting my gaze. "Hey."

They're usually pretty playful with each other, and I appreciate the exasperation Daphne shares on my behalf, but there's a tension between the two of them I can't miss.

Daphne's mouth is held tight, and her hands are pressed against her knees—instead of in the usual spot of being intertwined with Zoe's grasp.

"Everything good?" I ask lightly.

"Yep," Daphne answers as she turns back to the game.

Zoe does the same, but her expression is wide-eyed and a little giddy as she watches.

If our positions were reversed, Zoe would be unrelenting until I spilled whatever was on my mind, but unlike my best friend's need to dig in for details, I'm perfectly content to mind my own business.

I'm here to watch the game, and I'm going to try my hardest to actually pay attention.

Things aren't off to a great start, though, because we're already in the third inning.

I would have been on time for the start of the game if June hadn't come down with the flu suddenly, requiring Jessica to go home early to attend to her and leaving us short-staffed at work.

We also had a quick and impromptu celebration at the news that I won a handful of small scholarships I applied to —but we're still waiting on the news from the grant that will lock everything in and ease my worries a bit.

Lucas, of course, will be very forgiving of my tardiness, but he won't get my explanation texts until after the game is over because his coach forbids phones in the dugout—

apparently, he'd rather the team devote their time to spitting sunflower seeds and chewing massive pink wads of gum.

As if on cue, Daniel dumps a handful of seeds in his mouth, and I turn away before I can see what the end result of that is going to be.

Instead, I open my purse and pull out a brown paper bag where my own in-game treats are waiting for me—courtesy of Aunt Marie, who shoved it in my hands as I dashed out the door—and inhale the scent of warm butter and sugar.

She's been trying out new flavors, and this is the latest batch of cinnamon chocolate cookies, which smell absolutely divine.

"You snuck in food!" Zoe exclaims.

Her tone is somehow excited and accusatory at the same time, and I shake my head as I break off a piece.

"I don't think I've really been doing any 'sneaking' here," I argue. "I mean, there's no hulking security guards or snack police around. No one's double-checking that I *didn't* get these from that pitiful snack bar."

Zoe scoffs. "My hot pretzel with questionable lukewarm nacho cheese was actually pretty good, thank you very much."

I quirk a brow. "Oh, I'm sorry, did I offend the person who heated it up?"

"No, but you could at least *pretend* to be excited to be here," Zoe chides. "It's a playoff game!"

"I know. But I didn't realize you were so into all this. I thought Daphne was the only one out of the three of us who actually paid attention to sporty things."

Daphne sighs in exasperation, still keeping her gaze outward as the teams trade places on the field. "She's been like this since we arrived."

Zoe's nostrils flare at our retorts, then her eyes narrow in my direction. "I don't give a damn about baseball. I'm a *Kate* fan. And right now, your boyfriend is kicking ass at a sport he's played his entire life. Forgive me for being excited."

I grimace at her scolding, which is kind of deserved.

"I'm sorry," I tell her immediately. "I was just teasing. It's nice that you're here."

"Yeah, well, you missed a lot," Zoe says, miffed. "Lucas hit a double and *then* stole third! But the next guy struck out and left Lucas stranded. He's about to go up again, so you'll get your chance to redeem your watching."

I squint in his direction. "I thought Lucas was the best hitter on the team."

"He is," Zoe confirms.

"Then shouldn't he be going first?"

"From what I understand, the batting order has changed over the years. Like, it used to be that you try to put your best hitter as third and your best runners first so if there's a hit, you have a better chance for a run."

My eyes start to glaze over, and I have to force my attention on her words.

"But now, I guess, they're trying out different things, and I don't really know why you'd put Lucas second," she says. "Maybe it's strategic. I don't know for sure, though. You'll have to ask him."

"I will."

"If I learned that all in two tournament games, imagine what you could pick up if you actually tried," Zoe scolds.

I huff out a laugh, but I get her point and do my best to drum up some sort of interest in the gameplay.

I probably should have done this all along instead of reading or doing homework or hiding out in the hotel room in Erie for most of the tournament because I realize it's kind of a vibe.

It's a gorgeous sunny afternoon, and the scent of popcorn drifts over from the snack bar. Even though I stick to my own treats and reluctantly offer some to Daphne and Zoe, I can see the appeal of it all.

I watch the waves of hits, sprints, and catches, listening to the commentary of some of the people around us who are *really* into the game, and Zoe fills in the gaps when she can.

Each time Lucas steps up to the plate, there's an increase in the chants and cheers from our side—including people hollering his name—and boos from the opponents' stands.

But one voice in particular stands out from the rest.

It's deep and the loudest out of the crowd, and one look at the man makes me believe that this is without a doubt my boyfriend's father.

He stands with a tense posture each time Lucas's team is at bat, yelling critiques and calling for the umpire to change his mind on whatever call doesn't favor the team.

Also, he has the same exact build and side profile as Lucas, and I'm sure if I'd seen him years before his hair turned gray, he'd be a mirror image of his son.

I scan those around us, trying to pick out Lauren and

immediately get nervous at the thought of Lucas's parents bumping into each other here.

Thankfully, Lauren is nowhere to be found. I don't know if it's intentional that they're not at the same game, but I assume he'd swap his father for his mother in an instant.

The scowl on Lucas's face is unmissable, even from my vantage point a few rows up the bleachers, as his spot in the batting order comes up after Daniel hits and makes it to first base.

Lucas adjusts his helmet as he approaches the plate, and I think it has the same effect for him that wearing my headphones does for me—blocking everything and everyone else out.

He takes a few practice swings, then rolls his shoulders out before he gets into position, slightly hunched and ready to put the force of his entire body into the movement.

His hips sway as he waits patiently for the pitcher to wind up, and when the ball releases, Lucas swings.

I hold my breath as the ball cuts through the air, and the bat connects with it just enough to send it off to the side.

It's called as a foul, which doesn't seem like a big deal to anyone but Lucas's father.

"Come on, Lucas," his father yells, clapping his hands. "Pay attention to the pitch."

The murmurs and chatter die out once again as Lucas taps his bat on the plate, and his chest rises and falls in an exaggerated motion before he takes his stance again.

Before I can even register what happens, the pitcher snaps the ball over to second base, sending Daniel scurrying back to first after a failed attempt to steal, and he remains distracted, gaze moving between Lucas and Daniel.

The ball goes flying once again toward Lucas, who swings *hard* and misses.

"Strike!"

I wring my hands on my lap as the winces and groans pick up.

"Eye on the ball," Lucas's father calls sharply.

I scoot to the edge of my seat, willing the next attempt to fly in a perfect position for Lucas to smash it out of the park.

But when the blur of white is released, it's not toward Lucas at home—it's to second base once again where Daniel hurls his body. His hands slide forward and legs go up as he nears the plate, but the ball barely makes it there before he does.

He's signaled as out, but Daniel smiles and shrugs as he jogs back to where his teammates are waiting for him.

"Bad call," Lucas's dad yells.

I don't think anyone agrees with him, and I don't focus on him any longer because I'm now consumed by the ball of tension that is forming as knots in my stomach as Lucas eventually strikes out.

And it doesn't let up until the player after him suffers a similar fate.

"Maybe they should have had Lucas go first," Zoe says. "Or something."

"Maybe that guy should shut the hell up," Daphne adds, glaring at Lucas's father.

He grips the fence separating the field from the stands and yells a few choice expletives toward no one in particular, then turns back around, waiting for someone to back him up.

I don't really know a lot about this sport, but I understand enough that his dad is far too aggressive for the game —even if the stakes are high—and that he should sit down and be a passive audience like the rest of us.

As the teams switch positions on the field, Lucas stays behind for a beat, caught up in conversation with his coach.

I can't make out the words, but I sense the intention by the way Lucas's hands move as he speaks and the way his coach eyes the spectators warily.

Lucas grabs his mitt and jogs out as his coach also leaves the safe haven and moves around the field of play toward us, weaving his way toward Lucas's father.

"Mr. Hunt," the coach says, approaching with his hands up.

I think he's trying to signal that he doesn't mean any harm, but Lucas's father is red-faced at the mere sight of him.

Their body language narrates the exchange for me, with Lucas's father's temper flaring and the coach attempting to calm him down while directing him toward the parking lot, and it devolves pretty quickly.

He actually starts poking the coach in the chest to punctuate his sentences until a fresh round of expletives is unleashed between the two men.

"You're done," the coach yells, grabbing him by the arm.

And I watch, slightly gobsmacked, as he's escorted out.

"Holy crap," Zoe breathes.

Applause and cheers break out all around me, and I

frown at the collective enthusiasm that isn't directed to anything related to the game itself.

I, obviously, don't like any sort of attention, but I'm certain that this is the one type of it Lucas absolutely doesn't want. The thought of it gives me secondhand embarrassment, and I hope that he's able to shake it off and focus.

I'm only able to have eyes on Lucas for the rest of the game, who appears to be both sick and devastated in the wake of his father's conduct.

I, of course, can relate.

But I wish I didn't.

For Lucas's sake and mine.

SEVENTEEN

We're at the victory party, but Lucas radiates defeat.

If it weren't for the roar of the celebrations around us, it would have seemed like his team got destroyed in the latter half of the game, but it's the furthest thing from the truth.

In fact, Lucas played tremendously after his father was forced out, hitting a triple when the bases were loaded and securing the win in the seventh inning.

I definitely admire him for being able to maintain a level head and stay "in" the game, focusing on nothing but the steady rhythm of hits and catches because I absolutely wouldn't have been able to.

My go-to is hiding out by myself with a book and desserts, not excelling at physical activity in front of hundreds of people.

Part of me did expect him to unleash everything he was holding in once the final pitch was called a strike for the game or when it was just the two of us on the drive over to Daniel's, but I was wrong.

Lucas has been pretty even-keeled except for the smile and kiss of gratitude for my outfit and support, and now, he's just kind of quiet and introspective while sitting beside me on the couch.

I've been people watching for the past hour, and aside from the fact that I know Lucas is hurting, I haven't minded it too much.

The games and toasts are mildly entertaining to be on the sidelines for, but I have to keep forcing my gaze away from Zoe and Daphne in the corner, who seem to be having a very heated discussion of some kind.

I'm quite content to snuggle up beside Lucas because of how I feel about him but also because I've never had grandiose dreams about what it would be like to attend a high school party. I've always found the scenes depicted in movies and books glamorize frivolousness I've never had any interest in partaking in.

And I'm not about to start now.

Especially as Lucas's eyes focus on nothing in particular while his teammates chug their drinks.

They've set up this space as party central, dragging the dining room table in to play beer pong and flip cup and games I don't know the names of, and I jump at the sound of someone setting up a speaker to blare music from.

The noise of the bass mixed with the happy toasting makes me squirm, and it's worsened when everyone starts chanting the school's alma mater—of which I don't know the words to—and all the yelling and smells and movement trigger a sensory overload.

I tap my feet on the floor, needing an outlet for the

jitteriness that's overtaking my chest, and I pull my hair to cover my ears.

It's not effective enough to muffle the sound, so I lean against Lucas's shoulder, muting the sound from one ear and tugging on the lobe of the other.

"You okay?" Lucas asks, sliding his hand into mine.

"Are you?" I retort.

He blinks and glances around like he's awakening back into himself and where we are, then shakes his head as his eyes roam over me. "You're probably ready to get out of here."

I squeeze his hand before he can make any sudden movements. "I don't mind staying if you want or need to or whatever. This is your victory party."

He scans the room, assessing the debauchery that surrounds us, then shakes his head. "I'm not really in the mood to celebrate."

"I figured," I admit.

"You want to get out of here?"

"Um, yes?"

He smiles, but it's pretty flat. "Is that a question?"

There's no dimple or sparkle in his eyes or any emotion that I normally associate with Lucas at this moment, and I don't like it at all.

Lucas has been there for me without judgment and fail, and I don't think I'm reciprocating.

I know that we've moved beyond the outright goals of what we wanted from our fake relationship, but I'm suddenly finding a renewed purpose within the bounds of our *real* relationship—and that's to make him feel just as supported and cared for as I do with him.

"I'm ready whenever you are," I tell him genuinely. "If you want to stick around and be in the noise, I can take it. If you want to drink it off, I'll be your designated driver. If you want to run like hell, well, I'm not very fast, but I'll do what I can."

"Thank you," he says before he presses a kiss on the back of my hand.

And then he promptly stands up, pulling me with him.

"Let's get out of here."

I smile at his words as I reach for my bag, catching another sight of what appears to be a full-on bickering session between Zoe and Daphne.

I fire off a quick text just to give Zoe a heads up that I'm fine and heading out, which I doubt she'll get until later, and Lucas and I do our best to slip away unnoticed.

Daniel opens his mouth like he's about to call us out for sneaking off, but Lucas cuts him with a glare that silences him before he even gets a word out.

I let out a breath of relief when I slide into Lucas's passenger seat, adjusting to the sound of whatever bugs are out enjoying the rapidly cooling night air and the hum of the engine.

I watch the house grow smaller in the distance, courtesy of the side-view mirror, then turn to face Lucas, watching how he drives with one hand on the wheel and the other on my thigh.

"Do you want to talk about it?" I ask after a few minutes of silence. "What happened with your dad at the game?"

"No." Lucas gnaws on his lip for a moment. "Yes."

I chuckle at his indecisiveness. "Well, I'm here for you. I meant what I said at the party."

I'm trying to find the balance between wanting to leave the opportunity open but not push him into sharing, even though I'm secretly hoping he'll open it up and lay it all out.

"You know, I was thinking about what you said the other week."

"Oh?"

"About how you weren't sure about our direction since we don't have any drama to deal with between us."

"What about it?"

"Who needs conflict between us when we have so much family stuff to deal with?" Lucas asks a little sardonically. "Enough's going on with everyone else that it makes me really appreciate what we have."

I beam at him. "That's very sweet, but that's actually a good point."

"I have a few of them up my sleeve," he says.

"I hate books that just have argument after argument and the conflict that drags on," I tell him. "The author misses out on the opportunity to show their characters fully develop as people, both as individuals and together."

"I like that idea much better," he agrees.

I lean back against the headrest. "Me, too."

The corner of his mouth ticks up, signaling what I hope is him slowly working his way back to normal.

"So, to continue with that line of thought...let's say, hypothetically, if two people rise above a fake dating scenario, what might be the next step for them?"

"Well, it depends," I say. "Is there an established dynamic between them?"

"I like to think so."

"Any mutual interests?"

Lucas considers it for a minute. "Actually, not really."

"Uh-oh," I tease. "Sounds like trouble ahead."

"Nope, not happening," Lucas says, squeezing my leg.

His fingers hit at an exact spot where I am, apparently, very ticklish, and I do a combination of a shriek and a howl as I jerk away.

Lucas looks back and forth from me to the road, eyebrows raised in surprise at the sound that just escaped me.

I can't help the laugh that rolls out, and it has the very wonderful side effect of getting him to give me that genuine smile of his.

My slight embarrassment is definitely worth it.

"You've made me really happy, Kate," he says.

"I'm glad you can revel in my discomfort."

He shakes his head. "I mean it. Seriously. I don't think I would have handled what went down with my dad earlier half as well as I did without you."

"Really?" I question in genuine surprise.

"You don't give yourself enough credit. Everything you went through with losing your dad and dealing with your mom and planning for your future...I know you think you're a burden, but you're kind of an inspiration."

"I think I'm just stubborn enough to persevere."

I'm joking, but he's not having it.

"I mean it, Kate," Lucas presses. "I'm lucky to be with

you. To have picked you up on the side of the road and convinced you to be with me."

My only response to his very sweet declaration is to be stunned into silence and tug at the ends of my hair.

Lucas clears his throat. "Anyway, back to the task at hand."

"Right," I say as I straighten up. "I think it is a major problem that there hasn't been some sort of mutual bonding that isn't just each other. So, maybe, that can be something to work on."

"Fair enough. But, also, I think we should go on a date. It's time we've had our *real* first date. Dinner. Hand-holding. Talking. You know. Those sorts of things."

I don't know if Lucas remembers that he promised to plan an epic birthday date, but if he does, his opportunity is coming up to do so on Monday.

Not that I plan on reminding him or making a fuss over it.

Because right now, something as simple as a meal and a calm night of just the two of us sounds perfect.

"I can be agreeable to that," I tell him. "When are you thinking?"

"Now's as good of a time as any."

I lean over and press a quick kiss against his jaw, unable to help myself. "I'm in. What are you in the mood for?"

"How do you feel about Indian food?" Lucas asks.

"Very good in general, but I can only manage a few bites of spice."

"Okay. Noted. How about Mexican?"

I wince. "I'm one of those unfortunate group of people who hates cilantro."

"Wow," Lucas breathes. "That's terrible."

"I know," I say, frowning in agreement.

"How about sushi?"

"Never had it," I tell him. "It kind of blows my mind that people can just eat raw fish and live."

"I've never tried it either, and I don't think we should gamble with our lives on our first date."

"Probably a good idea. The third date, though, it's on. We can figure out how to use chopsticks and everything."

"What about noodles?" Lucas asks. "There's a new spot that opened up by my house that seems promising."

"I can do noodles."

"It's decided, then."

I thread my fingers in his. "Good."

As he accelerates us toward our destination, it's not lost on me that Lucas is still open and advocating for us when he has watched his parents' relationship fall apart.

I've seen plenty of my mother's boyfriends come and go, too, but it's nothing to me because I don't exactly look to her as a shining example of family values.

But that doesn't mean I don't feel for Lucas and what he's lost.

"I'm really glad we're doing this," I tell him.

"A date or our relationship?" Lucas clarifies, quirking a challenging brow.

It's a relief to see that our time together has erased the traces of sadness from his features, and I'm honored that I can have this effect on him.

"Both. It's nice to be *real* together, you know?"

"I do know."

"Even if we haven't gone about things traditionally. I

mean, ours isn't the typical, pining away...love story. No longing glances or casual hand-brushing."

"Like this?" He makes a big show of petting my hand like one would stroke a cat or a dog.

I let out a genuine giggle. "No. It's a thing from *Pride & Prejudice*. Well, the movie version, anyway, which is just as good as the book. Don't tell anyone I said that."

"Your secret is safe," Lucas assures me.

"Anyway, there's all this tension between Elizabeth Bennet and Mr. Darcy, and a lot goes into building their relationship, but it's the little moments that make all the difference. In one scene, he dares to touch her bare hand, which wasn't something people did at the time, and..." I realize I'm rambling and let out a sigh. "Well, I think you might have to see it to understand what I'm talking about."

Lucas tilts his head, like he's really trying to understand. "So, I was right...it *is* all about subtlety."

"Yeah, yeah," I relent.

"Is that stuff in other books, too?"

"Definitely."

"I think my perspective is skewed by *My Alien King*."

We both laugh at that.

"Well, in standard contemporary romance, there are subtle things the love interest might notice that add up to swoony moments," I explain.

"Interesting," Lucas says as he rubs his thumb along mine. "Like how you wear headphones when you want to block out the world around you?"

"That one's obvious, I think."

"What about the specific way you tie your hair back when you read? Or how you bite your bottom lip when you're measuring out milk for drink orders at work? Or how you always shift on your feet three times, left, right, left, when you're uncertain. Oh! What about the way you eat the perimeter of the entire cookie first so that your teeth marks make it look like a sun before you move in for the rest?"

I swallow. "Those are...less obvious."

"I am very aware of you, Kate. I have been since the start. When you crashed into me and my life in the library."

We idle at a stoplight, so he's able to say the next words while meeting my eyes.

"I wonder what you're doing when I'm not around. What you're thinking when I'm looking at you or talking to you. I'm trying to learn what you like and dislike. And to see you for who you really are."

Like in so many stories I've read, the only logical response to a declaration like that is to kiss him.

And so I do.

EIGHTEEN

The timer on my phone beeps, signaling that the boiling water has covered the noodles in the cup of Ramen long enough for everything to be soft and consumable.

It's definitely not going to be as good as what Lucas and I shared last night, but I like that now every time I reach for a little Styrofoam cup, I get to associate it with the mental image of him attempting to wrangle noodles at the restaurant.

That is to say that our first date was lovely and low-key, and it's one of many I hope we'll have together.

For now, though, I plan on curling up on the couch with my lunch and a book and just unwinding for a little bit.

As I get all settled into position with my legs at the perfect angle to balance my latest read and my cup of noodles, the doorbell rings.

The chime is pitiful, but it's unmissable, even though it's been years since someone used it.

I approach the door with trepidation, knowing that

anyone coming to see me would have probably called or texted ahead of time, but when I crack the door and see Zoe's face, I let out a relieved breath.

That feeling of ease instantly vanishes when I notice the mascara-stained tear streaks lining her face.

"What's wrong?" I ask, opening the door fully.

As an answer, she flings her arms around my neck and begins—or resumes, I suppose—sobbing.

"Daphne," she chokes out.

I rub her back as she lets it all out, babbling only somewhat coherently about her and Daphne having a big fight.

I'm not exactly surprised by this news because it looked like they were headed in that direction when I left the party last night, but it still takes me a full twenty minutes to get her to settle on the couch and give me the full story.

"You know how Daphne was, like, *surly* at the game yesterday?" Zoe hiccups.

"Sure," I reply.

I wouldn't use that exact word to describe her, but I'm not going to voice that thought.

"Well, she's been like that for weeks when it's just the two of us, and it all culminated into that big fight last night, and…" A fresh round of tears collects in her eyes. "We broke up."

"You did?"

"Yeah. We did."

"I'm so sorry," I tell her, reaching for her hand and giving it a squeeze. "That's awful."

"Beyond awful."

"I know you had so many plans."

"*So* many plans!"

"And you were really excited to go to prom together."

"Prom," Zoe whines and sinks back against the cushions.

"I'm sorry." I pat her upper arm as I apologize again. "I didn't mean to bring that up."

"It's just my reality. I mean, she couldn't have waited until we were done with prom and end of school stuff before deciding we needed to give ourselves space to 'find ourselves separately' next year and shattering my heart? It's going to be so miserable with the RA."

"I'll be there as a buffer," I say in reassurance. "You won't have to face her alone."

"Thanks," she says, sniffing. "You know, you're more *touchy* than you used to be."

I wince and put my hands in my own lap. "Sorry."

She shakes her head. "No, I like it."

"Okay," I say with a smile.

She watches me for a beat. "Lucas has been good for you, you know? It's been so crazy to watch you two fall for each other and have this cute little perfect romance. I can't believe that out of the two of us, you're the one ending this year in a great relationship."

I tug at the ends of my hair. "Well, it hasn't always—"

"God, that was so mean," she cuts in. "I'm just a jealous monster and an emotional wreck."

"It's fine, Zoe."

I mean what I say to her because I'm not going to hold her to everything she's saying at this slightly volatile state of existence.

But it's not actually fine.

Because the sound of the front door being thrown open

and crashing against the wall is enough of a jarring signal for me to jump up.

I know what that means.

"You'd better get out of here," I say quickly.

Zoe bats at her eyes as she balks. "What? Why?"

"Katherine, c'mere right now! NOW!"

My mother's words are slurred together so hard that I can only imagine what the state of the rest of her is.

Zoe perks up, ignoring my distress. "Is that your mom? She's home?"

"Uh-huh," I say, pulling her up by the wrist.

Confusion is evident in her pinched eyebrows as I tug her along, wondering how much of a fuss she would make if I forcibly shoved her out the back door.

"It's been forever since I've seen her," Zoe protests my dragging. "Let me say hello before I go home and cry for hours."

"That's not a good idea," I tell her. "Maybe some other time."

Zoe is my best friend in the world, and while she normally pulls whatever I'm thinking out of my mind, this is one thing she's never been privy to.

I've completely shielded her from what I go through at home.

It's not that I don't trust her with the information—because even though she's a gossip, she's still loyal to me—but I didn't want to subject her to it.

I also don't want pity or judgment, even the unintentional kind, more than I already dole out to myself.

Zoe, though, is determined to greet my mother before she heads home.

She gets out of my hold and strides into the hallway with the intention of starting a friendly conversation with my mother—which she has had sparingly few of over the years—but stops short at the way my mother is leaning on the wall for support.

"Hi, Mrs. Crawford," Zoe says politely.

My mother squints at her with one eye open. "Who are you?"

Zoe's gaze darts to me briefly before she lets out a tight chuckle. "Zoe, of course. Kate's best friend. You know?"

"Kate! Get over here."

I step forward, fully taking in my mother's disheveled appearance.

She's in a strappy, thin, and very short dress, and she's only wearing one shoe. Her mascara and lipstick are both smeared, which is nearly impossible to catch because she's swaying violently as she moves toward me.

"I'm so sorry," I say to Zoe. "But you need to go."

She gives me a wide-eyed nod before she slips out.

At the very least, it seems my nightmare of a reality has made hers feel a little less overwhelming.

"Mom," I say forcefully as she falls into me. "What are you doing?"

"What are *you* doing?"

Based on my experience, there are a few ways this could go.

If I help her out, she'll likely push me away or start screaming at me for trying to tell her what to do. If I try to reason with her, it'll turn into an argument. If I ignore her, she'll inevitably break down.

None of those options are ideal, so I go for what feels right at this exact moment—continuing on with my plans.

"I'm having lunch," I answer, then turn away from her abruptly.

I head back to the couch, resuming the position I fell into before I was interrupted.

"Don't walk away from me," she snaps.

I sigh as she steps toward me, spending more time trying to right herself than making actual movement.

"I'm not *walking* anywhere," I mutter.

I renew my grasp on my container of noodles as she stumbles over to the couch, hitting her shins against the side.

"How dare—"

She winds up her arm like she's about to throw a curveball, and I flinch away from the impact zone just enough so her palm collides with my lunch.

I try to recover the fumble as it happens, but I don't quite grasp it. The full cup lands on its side, sending noodles, water, and seasoning across the floor.

I'm glad that my legs are tucked up and I don't get to experience a Ramen shower on my skin, but the sight of a perfectly good meal—and so many other things in my life—ruined by her boils my blood.

The fury I've worked so long to suppress can no longer be contained.

I know it's not just the spilled noodles that send me over the edge—it's the culmination of my secondhand frustration with Lucas's father and Zoe's breakup and the fact that I just wanted to carve out a little bit of time for myself.

But I'm not going to get that or any form of peace if I

bite my tongue or spend another minute in my mother's presence.

"That's it," I say, tone venomous. "I'm done."

I think a past version of me would have retreated rather than stand my ground, but I'm a new and improved person these days.

I have less than twelve hours until I turn eighteen, and I don't have to put up with this anymore.

She follows me, at a much slower pace, as I head to my room.

"What are you doing?"

I pick up my book bag and hastily shove my few belongings and clothes inside it. "I'm leaving."

"No, you're not," she snaps.

I stop to look at her as I shoulder my bag, taking in the sight of the woman who has brought me nothing but pain, heartache, and anxiety issues for years.

And I'm done with her.

"Dad's been gone for a long time. Long enough that I forget the sound of his voice and the smell of his cologne. And I'm at peace with that." I step closer, hoping that she's able to focus and let the words sink in. "But what I will carry with me for the rest of my life, quite vividly, is the way you've made me live after he died. I will never, ever forgive you for that."

"Katherine," she says, blinking rapidly.

"This is the last time you're ever going to see me," I promise her.

She sputters as she leans on the doorframe for support. "Like hell you're going to—"

"No," I cut in sharply. "This is it. We're done. You're no longer going to have any control over my life."

It's wonderful to say those words out loud.

In fact, with my intention and declaration hanging between us, I feel lighter and more free than I ever have in my entire life.

I'm not sure whether the emotional upheaval is too much for her or the motion of her exaggerated movements set in, but her nails dig into the wood as she doubles over and promptly vomits all over the floor.

"Disgusting," I say, backing away from the sight.

She stays half hunched over with her greasy hair, and I debate slipping out the window to avoid her completely.

It might be guilt or the last remnants of feelings I have for the woman she used to be, but I find her pathetic enough that I'm compelled to help.

This, I think, is rock bottom for her.

I move her over to the bed, which, thankfully, she does without complaint, and I all but throw her on her side, careful of where I touch, then get the hell out of the room, the house, and her life.

I do hope that someday she can figure out how to accept help, but I can't let her drag me down any longer.

I'm moving on, leaving her dead weight behind—I'm facing the world on my own and taking control of my own life.

And it feels pretty damn good.

NINETEEN

"Kate!" Zoe calls down the hall.

I flinch at the sound of her voice.

Not only am I still feeling a little sensitive to raised voices right now but I've been counting down the minutes all day long to find out Lucas's plans for tonight—and he's in the parking lot now waiting for me.

"My birthday girl," she says brightly.

It's how she's greeted me all day, trying to mask her lingering sadness with her excitement over my "special day," as she calls it.

She, surprisingly, has brushed by every reference of yesterday's events—both my mother and the situation with Daphne—in an attempt to keep herself in a bubble of happiness.

I think it's a coping mechanism, and it's one I'm not going to judge her for or call her out on.

After all, I spent the entire lunch period with Ms. Molinaro doing deep breathing exercises and meditation, which was focused on manifesting the future and grant I desperately want.

Zoe smiles at me as she loops her arm through mine. "I have a little something for you."

"Oh, that's okay," I tell her. "You didn't have—"

"To get my best friend in the entire freakin' world a gift?" Zoe finishes. "Wrong. Well, technically, I didn't *get* you something, but I brought it for you."

She leads me into the bathroom and throws her massive purse on the counter.

"I don't know how you carry that around all day," I say to her.

"Come stand in the good light," she says, ignoring my quip.

I sigh as I move just where she wants me, and she digs through her purse, pulling out the materials she needs to get into mini-makeover mode.

She runs a brush through my hair, then dabs eyeshadow on my lids and a bit of mascara on my lashes before insisting I pull on a tank that exposes about two inches of my stomach.

"Zoe, this is too short," I say, pulling it down only for the fabric to move right back up.

"I don't have time or interest in your objections," she retorts as she stuffs the shirt I wore to school in her bag. "No need to argue. Just go off and have the perfect date."

I narrow my eyes at her. "You know what he has planned?"

She laughs before she pulls her fingers over her mouth in an exaggerated zip motion.

"Fine," I breathe, giving my appearance a once-over in the mirror.

"I did good," she says.

I nod as I look at the little bit of highlights over my skin. "You did. Thank you."

She throws her arms around me. "Happy birthday, Kate. You deserve to have the date of your wildest romance dreams."

"You do, too," I say as I pull back.

Her eyes drop briefly before she tucks a lock of hair behind her ears. "I'll find it someday."

"I know you will."

"Go on," she encourages, waving me off. "Call me later, though. I want all the details."

There's the Zoe I know and love.

"Of course," I promise before I head out.

I forgot to count how many steps Lucas's car is away from the front entrance earlier, but it feels like one million as I power walk as fast as I can without getting out of breath or disturbing my appearance.

When he picked me up from Aunt Marie's apartment this morning, I almost sobbed tears of joy at the sight of him with a mug of coffee and a donut with a candle in it.

I swear that for the rest of my life I'll be chasing the absolute glee I felt starting my day off with caffeine, sugar, and Lucas.

At least, that's what I thought at the time, but now, I somehow find his current state to be even more appealing —he's leaned up against the side of his car with a bouquet of flowers in his hands.

I've never been on the receiving end of this gesture

before, and while I think it's a little frivolous, I absolutely love it.

He stands up to his full height as he holds out the flowers. "Hey, birthday girl."

"These are gorgeous," I say, accepting them along with a quick kiss. "Thank you so much."

"They're also unscented," he says proudly.

I blink in confusion.

"I wasn't sure if you liked the scent of this kind of stuff. I know you're sensitive to perfumes and other things, so I thought about getting you a fake arrangement. But I looked online, and apparently there are 'odorless' flowers in the world."

I'm momentarily stunned by the declaration, but I come back to it enough to lean down and take a big inhale of the tulips and other blooms I don't recognize, confirming this information.

"That's really thoughtful of you, Lucas."

I don't know what I did to deserve him, but I'm absurdly grateful for him.

He smiles, showing off his dimple as he opens the door for me. "I'm trying to be more than thoughtful. I'm trying to wow you."

"You're well on your way," I tell him.

"Good."

I slide in and arrange my bag and the flowers on the back seat so they're stable, then rub my hands together while Lucas buckles in beside me.

"You look beautiful, Kate," he says, turning the keys.

"And you look very handsome," I return.

He always looks good, of course, but I can tell the little

details he's taken to clean up for the evening—changed his shirt, attempted to tame his hair, reapplied whatever gives him that light and very appealing spearmint scent.

"You ready?" Lucas asks, pulling us out of the parking lot.

"I'd be more ready if you told me what we were doing," I tease.

He reaches over and hooks his thumb in the hole on the knee of my jeans—the same pair from the first picture he posted of us. "You'll find out soon enough."

The way he turns isn't a route that I normally take or can associate to any destination, so I sit back and try to speculate on all the possible options.

And within about fifteen minutes, I have my answer.

"You brought me to a park?"

"I know you're not the outdoorsy type, but I think you'll like this," he says, excitement clear in his tone and on his features. "Come on."

For the second time today, I'm at the whims of the person leading me along, but in Lucas's case, it's on a paved path through a bank of trees.

I inhale the fresh air and appreciate the brief immersion in nature as we cut through it.

He swings our hands a little more than usual, and I take it as an outlet for his excitement, then start to feel the bubbly eagerness hit my own psyche as well.

"Just up ahead," he says as we near the end of the foliage.

"Okay."

I squint, guessing we have about twenty steps left, and I feel the anticipation drumming up with each one I take.

We're moving in sync, pace quickening to the point where we're both laughing and kind of jogging by the time we turn off and arrive at our destination.

"Lucas," I gasp, taking in the sight.

It's a little white gazebo tucked among the tall oaks, and it's the most adorable sight I've ever seen.

It's still early in the day—Lucas skipped practice, much to his coach's reluctance, to celebrate with me—but there is a set of string lights adorning the wrap-around railings, and a few balloons flank the entrance.

I tap them reverently as I step in, completely awed.

Lucas has created what can only be described as a nest of blankets in the middle of the space, but there's a screen and a projector set up as well.

"This is so cute," I say, smiling up at him.

"It gets better," he promises.

I don't know how it will, but I'm not going to question it.

I settle beside him in the middle of the cozy arrangement and watch him flip the lid on the cooler. It appears to be packed with items from Books & Beans, which means Aunt Marie picked my favorites, along with some fizzy drinks.

"Wow."

"And the essentials are here, too." He pops the lid on another box. "Take a look."

I lean over him, noting the very familiar book titles, which seem to be a mix of classics and a few modern favorites of mine.

"I do need to rebuild my collection," I tell him.

"You do, but I was thinking you could pick a book and

we could watch the adaptation," Lucas says, rubbing the back of his neck. "Follow along with the book and see what's missing, or we could just talk about it together or something?"

And I swear on everything good in the world that my heart actually swells in my chest.

"It's perfect," I tell him, turning to kiss him full on the mouth. "You're perfect."

He laughs and pulls back, much to my dismay. "There's more."

"You've already outdone every other birthday I've ever had."

"I like that I'm setting the bar for all your birthdays to come." Lucas smirks, running a hand through his hair. "Luckily I have a year to plan the next one."

I move to capture his lips again, but he shakes his head and reaches into the box of books and pulls out a very familiar title.

"There's no movie adaptation for *My Alien King,*" I tell him, laughing at the sight of it. "Unfortunately. I mean, the logistics of filming that would be interesting at least."

"I do know that, but still…" He gives me an expectant look as he presses it into my palm.

I quirk a brow. "You're giving this back to me?"

"Open it."

I press my thumb against the jacket to flip it open, expecting the usual boring title page with the name of the book and author.

But it's not just that black and white industry standard I receive—because beneath it in tiny but perfect handwriting is a note addressed to me.

I'm screaming internally as I speed read the words.

Kate,

I don't think your boyfriend is my target audience, but I'm honored that you brought him into the book world with one I've written. His note, which I'm keeping to use as inspiration for when I need to write a very swoon-worthy teenage heartthrob, was absolutely precious. You've got yourself a good one.

Happy eighteenth birthday!

Best,
Q. L. West

P.S. He also wants to know if you'll go to prom with him. (Say yes!!)

"Lucas," I say, voice thick with emotion.

"Kate."

"You are…" I pause to glance back down at the book. "I can't even think of a descriptor worthy of you."

"So, I'll take that as a yes? To prom?"

I nod as I reach for him once again to close the gap between us.

And this time, he's happy to give in.

TWENTY

"Thank goodness all the '90s styles are back," Aunt Marie says, looking over my shoulder at the mirror.

I smile at my own reflection, smoothing the silky blue material over my hips. "I can't believe you wore this."

She smirks at me, cocking an overdrawn black eyebrow. "That was before I found my own style. But it definitely works for you."

"I actually agree," I say, turning to the side to admire the simple cut of the dress.

I don't know the proper words for the actual style, but it's floor-length and kind of clingy all the way up to a high neck that cuts around my shoulders with thin straps.

Aunt Marie helped me with my hair and makeup, and even though it's a light coat of everything and a simple down and straight look, I feel stupidly glamorous.

And I don't mind it one bit.

The buzzer to her apartment sounds, pulling me out of my admiration.

"I'll get it," she says.

"Thanks," I return, bending down to slide into my borrowed low heels.

I touch up the lipstick a little bit before I join her in the living room—which also serves as my bedroom at night—and my eyes widen at the sight of Lucas in his tux.

"Wow," I breathe.

"I know, right?" Zoe says, coming through the kitchen to join us. "Cleans up nice."

I laugh. "So do you."

Unlike my somewhat retro appearance, Zoe looks like an ultramodern fashion model with her skin-tight red dress, high slit, and heels that put her well over six feet.

She flips her waved hair over her shoulder. "Thank you."

"Come on all of you, get in for a picture," Aunt Marie says, pulling out her phone.

The three of us pose against one of her many walls of art with me in the middle flanked by two of the most important people in my life.

We do a few rounds of pictures as a group before Zoe graciously steps out and treats Lucas and me like a fashion shoot, dictating how we should stand together and snagging Lucas's phone to take pictures for his feed.

It's a full-circle moment from when we sat on those bleachers and took that photo of his hand on my leg with the field in the background, and I smile as the three of us climb into his car and head off to the venue.

I thought that most schools threw big dances like this in the gym, but I've known ever since the fateful poster painting session that we've actually managed to score the ballroom of some fancy hotel in the city, meaning we have about a half-hour drive on a long stretch of highway.

We make it about halfway with no problems, just a lot of happy chatter and excited speculation from Zoe before she lets out a sigh.

"Can I put on some music? I need to get in the right headspace."

Lucas gives me a look like it's totally up to me.

"Can you keep the volume at a reasonable level?" I ask her.

Zoe rolls her eyes. "I am familiar with how you operate. But I really need some Lizzo to pump me up for this run-in with Daphne."

I wince. "Are you going to be okay?"

"Of course," she says flippantly. "She's been watching all of my posts since we broke up."

"What does that mean? That she wants to get back together?"

"Probably." Zoe doesn't glance up from her phone as she puts on one of her favorite songs. "But I'm over it."

I give her my best skeptical look. "Are you?"

She shrugs. "I will be. With time. I have the feeling that I'll find my own female equivalent of Lucas Hunt in LA this fall, so I'm not too worried about it."

Lucas laughs at her statement. "I'm honored that you hold me in such high regard."

"Don't let it go to your head," she says, smile tugging at the corner of her mouth.

"Wouldn't dream of it," he assures her.

"Well, there's nothing like a little hard labor before prom just to make certain of it."

"Hard labor?" I ask. "I thought all the pieces for RA are already assembled?"

"That's what Austin said," Zoe answers. "But Daphne lacks a certain sophistication, and without my vision, I'm sure the display is in shambles."

"I guess we'll see," I offer.

"We will," she says with certainty.

And we quickly find out when we arrive and step into the venue that Zoe was absolutely right.

What are supposed to be individual photo booth stations for people to meander through are currently arranged in a nonsensical way, ensuring that the flow of traffic through the displays doesn't make sense.

"Right, then," Lucas says, tugging off his jacket and tossing it over a chair. "How can we fix this?"

Zoe's nostrils flare as she takes in the scene. "You know what? Don't bother."

I balk at her words. "What?"

"Yeah," she says, letting out a low laugh. "I'm not going to let this get to me."

"But you've been planning this for months," I remind her.

"Oh, I've had *plans* all right." Zoe picks up Lucas's jacket and hands it back to him. "And since they're all in the trash, I've decided that I'm not going to let it bother me. I mean, if you can let everything go with your mom and Lucas can move on from his lifelong dream of being a baseball player, I can certainly not waste a perfect manicure and one single second fretting over this instead of enjoying the evening."

"It won't take me too long to move these, I don't

think," Lucas offers. "Besides, some of the team should be here shortly to help like they promised."

"And aren't other RA members coming, too? Aren't there supposed to be, like, string lights and other props here?"

Zoe presses her palms together and turns to face us both. "I appreciate the dedication, but seriously, I'm done. And I'm fine. This will not tarnish all the memories we're going to make tonight."

I wince at her cavalier attitude. "I mean, if you're—"

"We have the entire setup to ourselves right now," Zoe says, reaching for my wrist. "How about we take advantage of them?"

I don't even get a chance to answer before she's pulling me along.

"Lucas, do the honors, will you?" Zoe calls over her shoulder.

"Sorry," I mouth, handing over my phone.

He smiles. "No worries."

"Let's start with the floral backdrop because it will look so good with our dresses, then move on to the traditional photo booth," Zoe says. "Which is how *I* would have organized it, but what do I know?"

"Zoe," I breathe.

"Don't 'Zoe' me," she chides. "Just go with it."

Lucas laughs as she forces me to pose in the traditional prom style, and then when we slide over to the photo booth, she frowns at the currently meager selection of props, then offers me a pair of oversized sunglasses.

She goes for a cowboy hat, which, somehow, she manages to look incredibly chic in.

I feel a little awkward, but we stand side by side and blow kisses at the camera.

Lucas, very kindly, takes a few angles as Zoe and I break out in a fit of giggles, but mine fade as I look over the lens of my phone and see how his eyes widen at the screen.

"Do we look that ridiculous?" I ask him.

"No," he says immediately. "Of course not."

I take off the sunglasses and toss them on the table. "Then what is it?"

He shakes his head as he meets my gaze. "You got a notification reminder. I, uh, read it. Sorry. But I think you're going to want to do the same."

"What's wrong?" I ask, closing the distance between us.

"Nothing's wrong," he says.

I snatch the phone and take in what he has up—an email that I missed from yesterday with the scholarship information regarding the big New York state grant I applied to.

"I got it," I gasp.

"I know," he says proudly.

I blink as I look up at him and then Zoe. "I GOT IT! I got the grant!"

"YES!" Zoe screams before throwing herself at me.

I'm being dually embraced by Lucas and Zoe, and it's an incredible feeling knowing that my future is going to be okay.

I'm going to be okay.

Everything I ever wanted is ahead of me, and I can't wait to experience it.

Actually, I can.

I'm beyond content at this moment, happy to live my

own life and be in control of it while experiencing one of the final rites of passage in high school.

"PROM TIME!" Daniel's whooping voice calls across the room.

What looks like the entire baseball team and their dates, making up a big percentage of our senior class, follows him in.

Zoe steps away, still beaming at me, while Lucas wraps an arm around my waist to press a kiss against the side of my head.

We're quickly swept up in the activities of the school dance when the DJ cues up music that's a little too loud for me, but the energy of the room is incredible.

For the first time in my life, I feel like I'm a part of something rather than just having secondhand experience —either through observing the world around me or reading it in a book.

"Come here," Lucas demands, twirling me around so that I'm facing him.

The music has slowed down to some piano-based song I don't recognize, but I'm grateful for the interlude among all the hard rock and techno beats.

I slide my hands up, locking my arms around Lucas's shoulders as his palms rest on my waist.

We sway, slightly, among the other pairings—and I laugh lowly at the sight of Daniel and Zoe singing along and moving a little too fast around the space together, bumping into other people as they go.

"I can't believe this is my life," I tell Lucas, smiling up at him.

"That we're at prom on the brink of graduating, or that you're here with me?"

"Both," I answer immediately. "Who would have thought you bumping into me in the library would—"

"I think we agreed that it was a mutual collision?" Lucas cuts in.

"If that's what you need to tell yourself," I tease.

He shakes his head and smiles at me, and I stand on my tiptoes to kiss the dimple before it disappears.

"But, that said, I have to admit I was a little disappointed by the fake dating trope," I admit.

"Is that so?"

I nod as he pulls me even closer. "I mean, we failed pretty spectacularly at it."

"I'd say we both won at the end, though."

"I agree," I tell him seriously. "Because we've created a trope of our own. And I wouldn't have it any other way."

TWENTY-ONE

FOUR MONTHS LATER

Three stops on the train.

Followed by a short walk right through campus.

I haven't counted those exact steps yet—mostly because I'm just too excited to see Lucas that it's all I can think of the moment I step off the train in New Brunswick.

I suppose most college students don't spend every other Friday night hopping on a train away from the city after a weekly therapy session, but it's what works for Lucas and me.

We usually trade off who's going to scc who, but I expect the more we continue to settle into our routines and classes that we'll have actual plans to participate in.

But for now, we're content to do homework with each other, go for long walks around our respective campuses, and grab meals with our expanding social circles.

Lucas, even without playing baseball for Rutgers, has started to build a network of friends who he goes to the rec center with and can talk shop on the Pirates and the

Yankees and the Mets and the other teams whose names I have yet to retain.

While I do regularly video chat with Zoe, keeping up with all her adventures across the country, I've started to get to know the people in my dorm and classes. I've even been pleasantly surprised to find at least two other girls on my floor have the same appreciation for *My Alien King*.

I push through the entrance to the coffee shop, our designated meeting spot, and catch sight of Lucas immediately.

He's tucked away at a small two-person table in the back, and although this place doesn't have the same welcoming vibe as Books & Beans, it's a good substitute.

"Hey, you," I say as I approach.

"Hey," he returns. "I've missed you."

I settle in across from him, admiring that dimpled smile that still makes my heart flutter. "I've missed you, too."

"You okay?" Lucas asks, leaning over to kiss me.

When we first met, I absolutely hated that question, thinking I was projecting some sort of signal into the world that I needed to be worried about or pitied—but now, I welcome it.

Because I know what it truly means to be loved and cared for, and I'm happy to reciprocate it right back to him.

Before he can pull back, I hook my hand around the back of his neck, guiding him back down to me for a deeper and longer kiss, which he happily returns.

"Never better," I whisper.

And I mean it.

BOOKS BY JENNIFER ANN SHORE

Young Adult Romances

Everywhere, Always

Just for You

Just Play Pretend

Only You in Everything

Perfect Little Flaws

The Extended Summer of Anna and Jeremy

The Fake Dating Trope

The Stillness Before the Start

Adult Romances

In the Now

Nothing Personal for Breakfast

This Is Your Life

Young at Midnight

"The Islands of Anarchy" Series

New Wave

Rip Current

"The Royally Human Vampire" Series

Metallic Red

Yes, Your Majesty

FREE GIFT FOR YOU!

Want to make your book an autographed copy? Head over to Jennifer's website and get a free bookplate!

https://www.jenniferannshore.com/bookplate

CONNECT WITH JENNIFER

Hi there,

I cannot thank you enough for reading my work. Truly, it means the world to me!

I'd love to connect with you on social media if you're up for it. I'm on all the major social channels, including TikTok (@jenniferannshore) and Instagram (@shorely).

And don't forget to subscribe to my email newsletter (jenniferannshore.com/newsletter) for bonus scenes, new release announcements, giveaways, and more.

All my love! —Jennifer

ACKNOWLEDGMENTS

This book was therapeutic and fun for me to write in two ways:

1. I got to write about my sensory issues, which make me feel all itchy and retreat into silent solitude fairly often.

2. Talking through all of my favorite tropes and little thoughts I have about romance books and put them out in the world was a blast.

That said, this book wouldn't have been possible without so many wonderful people around me who help make the process "go," mostly giving me pep talks and reality checks whenever needed.

My editing team—Jen McDonnell, Denise Leora Madre, Emily Wright, and Lindsay Hallowell—consists of absolutely glorious humans who helped shape the story and the characters that are on these pages, and I'm very grateful for their perspectives and nudges.

On the visual side, Kelly Lipovich creates the most stunning covers that continue to amaze me every time I look at a stack of books, and Rachel Kilroy always photographs them so beautifully.

I have to give a massive thank you to all the book bloggers and reviewers who help spread the word about my books—I'm so lucky to have the loveliest advocates of my work!

Of course, my friends and family are the biggest advocates of all! I love you so much.

And, finally, to Christine, who I've dedicated this book to! Thank you for your friendship and very early support of my authoring career. I'm very grateful for our shared love of snacks, our pets, and vent sessions. You're the best!

ABOUT THE AUTHOR

Jennifer Ann Shore is an award-winning, bestselling author based in Seattle, Washington.

She writes romance stories that go a little deeper than the standard tropes. Her lineup of more than a dozen books includes standalones, a dystopian series, and a vampire series—with titles such as "Perfect Little Flaws," "Young at Midnight," and "Metallic Red."

Prior to publishing, she led an impressive career in New York, first as a journalist and then as a marketing executive, gaining recognition for her work from companies such as Hearst and SIIA.

Be sure to sign up for her newsletter on her website (https://www.jenniferannshore.com) and follow her on Twitter (@JenniferAShore), Instagram (@shorely), and TikTok (@jenniferannshore).

* 9 7 9 8 9 8 5 9 9 2 8 1 6 *